THE GODMOTHER AND OTHER STORIES

Also by Jan Lowe Shinebourne:

Timepiece
The Last English Plantation
Chinese Women, A Novel

THE GODMOTHER AND OTHER STORIES

JAN LOWE SHINEBOURNE

PEEPAL TREE

First published in Great Britain in 2004
Reprinted 2011, 2013
Peepal Tree Press Ltd
17 King's Avenue
Leeds LS6 1QS
England

ISBN 9781900715874

CONTENTS

For Zac, Clare and Tom
Zoe, Richard and Olivia

PART ONE

MEMORIES OF BRITISH GUIANA

Katherine Marshall, Toronto, Canada

Heat is bad before that kind of rain. Sweaty. Like hands on you. You put on fresh clothes in the morning. By midday it soak with sweat. The fruits cook up in the heat, get too ripe, drop: purple jamoon, orange arawa, yellow mango, white starapple, brown sapodilla, red sorrel. All the skins just burst like bombs. All the juice just running like paint in the grass, with the rainwater like glass in the grass. My whole garden wash away. The trees get sick and die. All the lettuce, the pepper, the thyme, the corn all go to waste.

In nineteen sixty-one I was starting to plant them back. I went with Fred to Agricola in the Land Rover. We use to pack all the young trees in the back then drive down the highway with them. That Indian boy from Berbice help me plant them in. What was his name? Harold.

In nineteen sixty-three you could not go anywhere. The streets were high up to your knees in water. The buses and car engines flood. At night I used to hear the fruits fall through the rain. The rain was like a river on the roof. It burst the gutters. I used to think – God, when this rain will stop? At Stabroek and Bourda the hucksters had to dash away the fruits in the Demerara River and Lamaha Canal.

Laurie had to wear galoshes to go downstairs and get in the car to go to school. Then the schools had to shut. Flu and arthritis break out – damp get into people head and feet.

Later, the papers print:

> *One of the members of the family was seen to climb out of one of the windows of the upper storey and stand on the ledge. The crowd below encouraged him to jump and made a ring of entwined arms but the boy shook his head and returned to the blazing room. Later his charred body was discovered near the window. He was Lawrence, the youngest member of the family who was due to sit his General Certificate of Examinations the following day at Queen's College.*

You know, I talk to Laurie. I say to him, "I know why you did it. Daddy was dying in the next room. He was talking to you from behind the wall on the other side. You went back to die with him. You went back to talk to him while he was dying. You did not want to leave him. Give me a dream, Laurie. Tell me the truth. No one is to blame, only history. You lived as long as God wanted. The Lord giveth, the Lord taketh away. According to Hindus, fire purifies the soul. You were purified in the fires in British Guiana in 1962. You went to heaven. But Hell came to Georgetown. Hell, bombing and murdering."

So much rain in sixty-three. Wash the whole of Georgetown. August was the wettest month. June and July was the nightmare, but August fling the rain in my face, as if to say, "Too bad it didn't rain on June 24th". The top floor of the house was cool. That was where Harry went to rest. Not only that night. Any time one of us was ill, the top floor was the place to go. The odours from the ground dispersed in the breeze so it is always clear air up there. Georgetown is not a city of tall buildings. Our house was one of the tallest. The trouble was, the fire cut us off in those rooms and to this day I can remember thinking if only we didn't live in that big house, if only it was a little cottage we could have all jumped through the windows and all lived.

Frederick Marshall, Toronto, Canada

To be the Harbourmaster is to train the binoculars on the warships. But to see them is to see yourself young again, ten years younger. Everything that was happening at this very moment – the burning city, the heat of the flames hotter than the afternoon sun, the rioters in the street below, the whole frightening scene – might as well be history already.

This time, this year, 1962, second time, second chance to blow up the two warships full of bombs, guns and rifles – full of white soldiers packed like cockroaches in the hold. Bring them in at twenty knots. They were not to know the speed limit or the shallowness of the bar. Sandbank them to the north of the city, by the Groyne. Hope that the fire spread to the waterfront and one by one, destroy each wharf, first Bookers, then Weiting and Richter, then Transport and Harbours, Rice Marketing Board, then the Esso storage tanks. A good, big explosion there would take burning diesel and petrol out to the warships and the bombs. How many in the ships could die? Three, four hundred? Pray no more Guianese would die, not by the fires, not at each other's hands.

The telephone is ringing. 14.05 hours.

"Harbourmaster Frederick Marshall here."

"Sir Ralph Grey, Governor here. HMS *Wizard* commanded by Commander D. J. Farquharson and the HMS *Troubridge* commanded by Commander T.A.Q. Griffiths are standing by and will be radioing for assistance.

"Yes, Excellency."

"Expected time of arrival at Sprostons No. 1 jetty?"

"16.45 hours, Sir, at high water."

"Can you bring them in earlier than that?"

"No, Sir."

No manners, nothing in the end from them. Not even an excuse-me to explain the reason for keeping anybody waiting. Never.

"Inform the commanders that a Lieutenant-Colonel Warren of the 1st Royal Hampshire Regiment is on his way from Atkinson Field with one rifle company in several vehicles. Also inform Lieutenant-Colonel Warren that the first elements of reinforcements from Jamaica will arrive in Georgetown at 19.00 hours, with more to come tomorrow from the 1st East Anglian Regiment, and the 1st Duke of Edinburgh's Royal Regiment."

"Yes, sir."

There is the telephone, next to the logbook. The clock is ticking faultlessly. Telephone Jagan. Get him to send people out. A small boat could get out there, pour petrol on the water, return to the shore, and set fire to the warship. They would never return to British Guiana again. Fumigate them.

You go to sleep at night, you wake up in the morning, but history never sleeps. Just like the logbook lying in the box under the bed for almost ten years. Fish it out. 1953. The whole thing is happening all over again – warships and troops again, just like 1953. The governor in 1953 was Savage, another one to turn you into a traitor and thief in your own country. In 1953, walking three steps behind him, any man could have picked up the piece of paper that fell out of his pocket, and kept it, never to return it. When afterwards the newspapers reported the lost document, and later the BBC World Service broadcast that the warship was heading for Guiana, it was good to paste it the logbook with the diary entry for 9th of October, 1953, and continue to use the same logbook, fetching and carrying it with this lunch box every single day to work, then when it became obsolete after three years contrive to report it lost, but take it home and hide it in the chest under the bed. Sleep on it night after night for nine years. All the nine years Maria stay married to that damn Englishman in England. Never to look at it or think about it again, until today, now that this document of history is going to repeat itself.

Lashley's son, the one who used to court Marilyn, and is now Assistant Manager at the radio station, is on the air: "Georgetown is haemorrhaging. Water Street is on fire. The Prime Minister's house is under siege. The Police and Volunteer force are trying to contain the disturbances."

Governor Grey telephones this morning, personally to ask for the warships to be brought across the Demerara bar because he cannot trust anyone else to do it like me in 1953. Why should I care about Governor Grey's trust? Or any other British governor? What do I care for dressing in this old Harbourmaster uniform, to have to drag it from the trunk from under the bed, and fish out the old logbook to bring it here today to Sprostons Wharf?

Open it. 9th October 1953. They rubber-stamped "Top Secret" across it in three places. The British Minister of Foreign Affairs signed it and stamped it with his Whitehall address. A self-important little piece of paper from a self-important little man from a self-important little country. They send their mercenaries around the world to dictate their orders and commands. They wear their trappings, their uniforms. They rule with their bureaucracy and rituals. They send their spies and saboteurs to set fire to our country.

The memorandum is creased but smooth, like an old

man's face. Here I am reading it again in the moonlight and by the light of a kerosene lamp falling in an arc across the page. I read it for the second time in a lifetime:

9th October 1953. 4 a.m. Two frigates each with 170 troops and shore craft with 100 troops. Superb *RM detachment on way inshore.*

Para two. Information from shore is that all is quiet.

Para three. CCA has gone on in frigate.

Para four. Superb *remains to seaward and will unload stores as weather permits.*

Para five. Hope to know soon whether frigates will be required to proceed to McKenzie and Berbice.

Para six. HM troopship Cheshire *sailing from Liverpool on 14 October reach Jamaica by 26 October.*

1st Battalion Gloucester Regiment to Jamaica as theatre reserve for Caribbean area. Unless emergency arises in British Honduras...request a battalion from British Honduras from where withdraw Royal Welsh Fusiliers for British Guiana...War Office considerable backlog troops for Far East...due movement Indian troops to Korea.

Para seven. Argylls embarking 8 and 9 October in HMS Implacable *for British Guiana*

Para eight. Troops will protect Governor and Europeans. If both, original plan as in Commander Caribbean Area 060243 to War Office will be carried out. Commander Caribbean Area will himself transfer to frigate for run-in, weather permitting.

Para nine. Airlift has been advanced as far as possible, expected time of arrival not yet known.

They could not have come in without my help. Those ships would have run aground. Today, nine years later, news of the warships came on the 12.15 B.B.C World Service News, and at 1.30 the Governor broadcast it on the local station.

The radio signal comes and there is another English voice:

"HMS *Troubridge* to Harbourmaster... are you receiving?"

"Harbourmaster to *Troubridge*. Receiving loud and clear."

"Request instructions to proceed into harbour."

"Harbourmaster to *Troubridge*. Advise you wait until 1445 to proceed into harbour. Highwater at 1449 hours will guarantee safe entry by 1530."

16.35 hours.

"HMS *Troubridge* under Commander T.A.Q. Griffiths, R.N and HMS *Wizard* (Commander D.J.Farquharson, R.N) has arrived outside the bar of Georgetown Harbour."

16.45hrs

"HMS *Troubridge* has entered the Harbour and secured alongside at No.1 jetty and will immediately despatch an Internal Security Platoon to Police Headquarters."

17.05 hrs

"HMS *Wizard* secured alongside HMS *Troubridge*. Despatching an Internal Security Platoon to the power station."

Now, far across the bar of the Demerara River, two British warships are waiting for me to navigate them into Sprostons Harbour. Train the binoculars on the warships and see once more their coiled steel hulk, too heavy, too impenetrable, for such a transparent sky and a river as shallow and muddy as the Demerara. I don't need any binoculars to see that Water Street is on fire, to see my own home, my own city on fire, to see rioters in the streets, and the warship on the river with more soldiers in the hold. Here on the bridge I have power to let the soldiers pass or not. The moment is now. It is here again, after nine years. By the time the soldiers reach the harbour, the whole wooden city, the people too, will perish.

HAROLD

All day, there were the same announcements on Radio Demerara: *Cheddi Jagan's People's Progressive Party has won the elections*. Every bus arrived with news that Cheddi Jagan himself was heading this way in a motorcade. So people began to leave the factory and canefields early, and stream home to wait for him.

Like masquerade, you could hear the crowd long before you see it – voices like flocks of birds crying and croaking in the distance; feet like cows' or horses' hooves beating the earth far away. Then when it rounded the corner you could see it was human.

The motorcade was a swell of chanting people. Drivers blared horns, cyclists rang their bells, Cheddi Jagan, a garland of flowers round his neck, was standing in an open car with his arms open. The chanting was intense near him, rippling out in waves.

"Down with the British!"

"Long live Cheddi!"

"Long live freedom!"

"Down with imperialism!"

"Down with masters!"

The more he waved and smiled, the louder they shouted. His car began to drown in the rising tide of bodies. They raised their fists, shook hands, blew kisses, waved hats and handkerchiefs. Many danced like drunken youths at a wedding. The more euphoric the celebration grew round him, the greater the frustration of people cut off from him. In their desperation to get closer, some jumped off the crowded bridge into the canal and swam to the other side.

From his house landing, the scene was clear for Harold to see, and hypnotising like a film. Right in the middle of it was Selena. She was leaning right on Cheddi Jagan's car. Jagan's wife, Janet Jagan, was in the back, and flanking her were two men dressed in the People's Progressive Party's youth uniform: green berets and red sashes printed with the large black letters, *PPP*. They were just like Fidel Castro and Che Guevara. One of them was flirting with Selena, and she was flirting back, looking him in the eye, smiling at him. Two other lieutenants were leaning from the car and cautioning the crowd, but it did not stop them sweeping Cheddi Jagan onto their shoulders. From this perch, he continued to wave and laugh. Men and women nearest him kissed his feet. The rest continued to blow him kisses and raise clenched fists.

Harold ran down the stairs, plunged through the crowd and pushed his way to Selena. Now, she was not admiring the lieutenant, but Janet Jagan who was laughing and shaking hands with the crowd just like her husband. When Selena saw him, she became hostile, so he pretended to ignore her. He offered one of the lieutenants a cigarette, with the word, "Comrade?"

Later, when it was over, some said a Bookers helicopter came to take the Jagans and their lieutenants back to Georgetown. Some said it was a lie, that like good communists, they drove themselves back to Georgetown.

★ ★ ★ ★

Later that night, Harold visited Selena. Her brother, Bender, was sitting on their veranda.

"You like the motorcade?" Bender asked.

He lit a cigarette. "Where Selena?"

The kerosene lamp indoors did nothing to lighten the darkness outdoors. He longed for Selena to appear but only the thick, cool leaves of the mango tree that grew close to the house rustled in his ears and filled his nostrils with perfume. They smoked, listened to the distant barking of a dog and glanced towards the dim streetlight at the end of the path, hoping to catch sight of one of their gang. Scaramouche and the others would be hanging around somewhere, at some culvert, or someone's house, wherever a family might tolerate their boredom and insolence.

When Selena did appear at the window, it was to shout at Bender.

"Bender!"

"What?"

"Make yourself useful. Go, buy Dad cigarettes."

She flung the purse at him hard, but he caught it.

When Bender shut the gate and was on his way along the path, Harold coaxed her. "Come out here and sit down."

She resisted.

Everything, he felt, people and circumstances, conspired to frustrate him when it came to Selena. It was too dark to see her face.

"The Jagans great people," she declared.

"Yes. You going to the fair next week?"

She sucked her teeth, not interested in talking about something so frivolous. She was still full of the Jagans and their motorcade. Soon, she left the window to come to the veranda and sit in the opposite corner. His heart raced, his mind stopped. He put out his right hand cautiously and touched her shoulder.

She slapped his hand away and hissed, "You mad?"

He replaced his hand. Now she sat as still and quiet as a bird.

"Look, Bender coming," she warned.

He searched the path. "No, Bender not coming." He moved closer.

When Bender opened the gate, she returned indoors. He was content with the hurried lovemaking that passed between them.

Bender informed him, "Scaramouche and the boys at the high bridge."

"Doing what?"

"Thiefing cane. Waiting to see if the white priest going to come to see them."

★ ★ ★ ★

They headed for the high bridge. For security, the canal was lit up all night, to safeguard the punts of cane. In the punt below the bridge, Scaramouche and his gang were sprawled out, feasting on stalks of cane, stripping off the skin with their teeth. They sucked the stalks dry and barefacedly threw the wasted shreds over the sides, leaving evidence of their raid floating in the canal and strewn on the banks. Harold and Bender swung themselves over the bridge, jumped, and landed among them. The younger ones rushed Bender to wrestle with him. It turned into a battle, with kicks and punches being exchanged. Bored, Harold sat down, chose an unblemished stalk of cane, and began tearing the skin off with his teeth.

Scaramouche tapped him on the shoulder with a stick of cane and asked slyly, "How Selena?"

"Mind you own damn business!"

The spotlights were clustered on poles on both banks of the canal. The beetles went mad near the bulbs, crashed into the heated glass and fell to the ground. Out of the graveyard of the dead and half-dead, some struggled to life again and flew upwards to rejoin the holocaust round the bulbs. Moths and sandflies floated in the fluorescent air. In the strange, artificial light, the grass and bushes on the banks looked plastic. The bulbs were so much brighter than daylight, it sucked the naturalness from the landscape, made the bare earth look hard and grey as concrete, the buildings like props that could easily collapse in the dead air.

Scaramouche was ringleader. He was older, bigger, tougher, ruder, and already a hard drinker. He made their business his, and now he asked Harold, " You follow the motorcade?"

Harold answered in his own time, "Yes."

Scaramouche boasted, "I follow it since it come from No. 19 Village, all the way."

"Madman."

Scaramouche laughed and prodded Harold's ribs with the stick of cane. "Madman? Me?"

Harold pushed away the cane.

"Mind you," Scaramouche continued, "I might join the Party one good day. They talk about improving this and that." He prodded Harold again, "Ask Selena. I think she might join too. She love them lieutenants."

A hoarse voice came from the bridge. It was the watchman, Vincent.

"Clear out, clear out from here!" He was wearing his security helmet. The spotlights made his face shine, the sheen on his khaki uniform glow, his helmet glint. He looked menacing, like soldiers in the films at the cinema. He ranted, "You got nothing to do? You know you can't eat the blasted cane?"

"Vincent," Scaramouche soothed. "We can't eat some cane now and then?" He stood up, holding his cane like a spear. His shirt was unbuttoned and hung open, exposing his hairless chest. His trousers were rolled up to his knees, and sagged with water.

"You know blasted well you can't eat no damn cane."

"We cut the cane whole blasted day in the hot sun. We eat the cane when we cut it. Why we can't eat it now?"

"Rules is rules!" Vincent screamed, hoarse. "Move your backside now." His hand went to the gun on his hip.

Mouthing curses, they jumped off the punts.

As they approached, Vincent turned to face them. He kept his eyes on Scaramouche who was still carrying the stick of cane. He passed so near Vincent he could have prodded him, as he did the boys when he wanted them to pay attention.

When Vincent was satisfied they were leaving, he mounted his bicycle, overtook them, then vanished in the darkness.

Out of the same darkness came a small light, like a round ball, coming towards them. No one moved. Perhaps it was an overseer, or one of the English soldiers. An engine sounded, perhaps a jeep, or an army truck. They waited. It was no use running. Whoever it was, could see them in the light: exposed, clutching sticks of cane and soaked from trespassing in the canal.

It was the priest, Father Mason, on his Vespa. Scaramouche laughed with relief, flagged him down and straddled the centre of the road so the priest could not pass. Harold began to walk away but Scaramouche grabbed his arm, and ordered him to stay and earn himself some dollars. Harold punched Scaramouche hard, but not hard enough to topple him. Scaramouche grabbed Harold from behind, around the neck, and pinned his arms back. The younger boys egged on Scaramouche who was not fighting in the usual way, not exchanging punches and kicks, but trying to paralyse Harold and trip him. They fell together. Scaramouche yelped in triumph. Harold fought to escape. Scaramouche was very strong tonight. Harold could feel he could not escape. For a very long time they rolled around in the dust from one side of the road to the other, Scaramouche fixed to Harold like glue, like a man to a horse.

Harold began to feel sick, weary, and faint. He became limp as a rag in Scaramouche's arms and blacked out. When he recovered, Scaramouche was lying beneath him, face up, and he was lying on his back, on Scaramouche, still imprisoned in the grip of his arms and legs. His eyes could see nothing except the tears of shame swimming all over the sky. There was no more pounding in his brain. The other boys were gone because he could not hear their voices. The light from the priest's Vespa was shining on them. The priest was standing over them, looking at him with his blue, blue eyes. Harold became aware that he was no longer clothed, that he was completely naked to the priest's gaze.

JACOB

This is my last day here in Georgetown Hospital. The end of another journey. If London was my first journey, this must be my second. The Prime Minister, Mr. Burnham, says we must come home and build Guyana. He wants only local culture, local music, nothing classical. He is banning everything foreign, but I am foreign now, my music is foreign.

They say travel broadens you. I lived six years in England. Before that, I lived twenty-four years in British Guiana, on a sugar estate village in Berbice. Those days, every Sunday I went to the Anglican Church. Monday to Fridays, I went to the Anglican school. Saturdays, I learned to be a carpenter and make furniture – my father's trade. He inherited it from his father. I remember the faces of my father, my mother, my grandmother and a few others. Otherwise, I can't relive my childhood, not in my memory, not in my feelings.

However, I do know that while I made, polished and repolished furniture in that stretch of villages in Berbice, I really wanted to study classical music. Mr. Sam used to play the church organ and piano. I can't remember how he came to teach me to play the piano, and how I came to pass my piano exams so quickly, but the English priest thought I was gifted, and I ended up taking lessons in New Amsterdam, later winning the national prize and a scholarship to study in London. It was too long ago to remember more clearly than that.

I do remember that Mr. Sam died. I remember his funeral. I remember how his relatives dismembered his house. So soon after he died, they took away his piano on a cart. I could not find another teacher in Berbice like him. The priest said I would find the best teachers in England.

In colonial days, a man who went to England was Christ in the virgin's womb. Returning home, he was Christ born. A man like me goes to London and thinks he's in England but London is a world by itself.

My first year in London, I remember above every other feeling, the feeling of cold. The next feeling I remember is loneliness. In my village, I was a loner because I was an artist, but never felt lonely. In London I stopped being a lone artist. I became only lonely. Yet, in London, I met the whole world. I met Africans, Indians, Chinese, Arabs, French, Italians, Germans, Greeks, Spaniards, Jews, Japanese, West Indians, other Guyanese. Yet, when I try to remember them as individuals I become as a man walking past an endless queue of dummies, each plastic with one expressionless dummy's face. This is how I met the whole world in London, the centre of the world. I remember travelling in the underground trains during the rush hour. There, all the people of the world were jammed against each other, in their minds trying not to touch each other, though their bodies were touching – blank-faced, silent, reading newspapers, trying to focus their eyes on the advertisements on the ceiling. How can the world see, yet not see each other? It was a shock.

I remember the music college, a formidable building with formidable paintings of formidable musicians. In every room and corridor, the paintings lined the walls. I can't remember learning music. I spent all my six years in a London nursing home among English patients, nurses and psychiatrists, then they sent me home, to this hospital in Georgetown, Guyana.

It could be said I ended my second journey the day I left London, England. It could be said I started a third journey the day I arrived at this hospital in Georgetown, Guyana. It could be said, but I would not say it. I feel I have never moved.

I lived one year in this hospital with three other patients in Ward Three: an old man who told obscene jokes; a convict manacled by his feet to his bed who played solitaire with a pack of cards, each one stamped 'Government Property'; and a man dying slowly of cirrhosis while his daily visitors come to wait for death with him.

Now here I am, waiting to be discharged. Mr. Forbes Burnham, I have come home.

Three fat women are sitting as if anchored to the plastic chairs. Their bellies are mounds of fat. They fan themselves with handkerchiefs and look mournful and sorry for themselves. An old East Indian woman in a white sari keeps going outside to spit in the flowerbeds. The sari does not hide her thinness. She looks like a ghost.

Two children keep running in and out of the room.

A thin old man is sitting opposite me. His whole body shakes except his immobile face. I have aged, not in time or years. I withered inside and grew fat outside.

I don't care. I don't feel like caring. I can't bear to care. Today is my last day here. The end of my third journey? I'm on the verge, the threshold as they say, of another? A fourth?

Once, I used to believe in psychiatrists, but they are like any doctor. What are people to them but loads to be carted from ward to theatre, from theatre to ward, like earth on a donkey cart? They all ask the same questions. The questions are set like examination questions, and so are the answers:

"How can you say you have not lived for six years?"

"Because I have felt nothing."

"Haven't you felt loneliness, haven't you felt cold, haven't you felt warmth, haven't you felt anger?"

"Yes."

"Then you have been alive!"

"No, I have felt nothing I wanted to feel."

"What have you wanted to feel?"

"I don't know."

The nurse is calling me, "Come Teach."

They call me *Teach* here in Guyana, because I wear a suit all the time. It's the only clothing I possess. I speak the Queen's language. It's the language I've been taught to speak.

The doctor's room. He does not look up. He is writing my certificate of health. He asks me how I feel. It's a rhetorical question. I say I feel fine. He continues writing. The doctor is a young man. We belong to different generations. *Generations*. I was talking with two high school teachers: University of the West Indies graduates. They are very proud they did not have to go to England for their education. They think it makes them better than me. They called me *colonial*. They said I belong to a different generation. *Generation*, *colonial*. Words. Do they really know what these words mean? People use these words like labels. They label you because you lived in a certain space and time. I wish I could even feel I lived in a certain space and time. I do not feel like a colonial. I do not feel like a nationalist like these new university graduates. I feel like a man floating in an infinity of space.

The doctor hands me my certificate of health. "You are a well man, Mr. Paul."

Well? Who is to say who is well and who isn't? I suppose I must go now. Where am I going? To what place? Back home to Berbice? Back, back, back, back. I know only ghosts there. It will remind me of my youth. It will remind me of my father and mother. What are they to me but ghosts? Silent ghosts in life and death. When we were together, we said little to each other. I was born in silence and I have lived in silence. I thought music was the only way to break this silence, not the words of history and politics. I can't remember because of this silence. Shame and silence. Shame and silence. Shame and silence.

Each Sunday morning they dragged me to church, literally. My mother used to tie me in a sugar sack, and drag me through the village to church. I hated church. I hated the noise of prayer. I did not feel holy. I felt humiliated. Come Sunday their voices broke, melted into a congregation of voices praying for a King and a Queen and to saints I did not know. All those Sunday mornings spent praying in that weary Anglican Church, flaying always in our faces the tattered red, white and blue of the British flag. As they prayed, their faces were blank. I prayed too. I muttered words we could barely speak, much less understand.

Why did I come back? Just because Forbes Burnham says everything is going to be all right? I feel like a man standing at the top of a staircase wondering whether I should go down. Going to London was reaching the upper rung of that ladder, then I had a breakdown. If I climbed up a ladder, then I can climb down. I am climbing down. The Anglican school is still there in Berbice. Perhaps I can teach there.

"Pull yourself together, Mr. Paul."

It is the doctor speaking. He calls the nurse.

The nurse wants me to leave.

"Teach, Teach, man, is what happen to you? A big man like you crying so? Man, Teach, look, look."

The nurse hands me my suitcase.

The hire cars are milling around the hospital gates. It's visiting hour. I think I'll walk to the car park. I love these shady avenues. I love these trees. I love being in the shade then coming out of the shade and feeling the sun warm my body. I see people. I see the shapes of houses and trees. I see light and sun. Here walking on the street I can feel the sun on my back. From today, I will be able to feel the sun on my back every day. The trees filling the avenue are beautiful with colour, beautiful in the shade or in the sun. The blue sky is beautiful too, full of beautiful white clouds. The light is pure. In this light, it is possible to see every colour that exists. I can feel the breeze splashing my face like cool water. It dries the hot, salty tears on my face. My name is Jacob. I live in the twentieth century. I live in Guyana. But the space I live in – looking at it defies boundaries and time.

The Berbice car park.

"Car, Sir?" a man is asking me.

"Yes."

Twelve years ago, he would have known me and I him.

I am the only passenger in this car as it heaves, dips, bends, falls, noses forward to that mirage watered by the sun. If I close my eyes the mirage will melt and melt it does as we draw closer and wipe it away.

The driver is asking, "Where you going, Sir?"

"Berbice."

"Which part?"

"Cumberland."

"Which part?"

"Second Street."

"Second Street is where I live! I am Persaud. Which house is your house?"

"The first house on the right."

"The brown house?"

"Yes." He smells of rum.

"It lock up long. You been away?"

"Yes."

"How long?"

"Eight years." It's a lie. "Seven years abroad, one year here. I was ill."

"You get better now?"

I pretend to be asleep.

I am awake. We're on the ferry. The noise of the boat's engines throbs in my ear. The driver is standing in front of the car with a group of men. They talk and laugh loudly; with a lot of backslapping and gesticulating. The lower deck is jammed with cars. In the old days, people used to be jammed in between the cars because there were not so many cars then. Driving out of the boat now I see people walking down a stairway attached to the upper deck. In the old days everyone exited through the lower deck.

The car sails through the crowd. It enters New Amsterdam. Nothing has really changed. It's getting dark. By the time we reach Cumberland, it is impossible to see anything except the feeble lights from the lampposts; they glow in the sky and illuminate the tops of the trees.

"Second Street, Sir."

I pay him; I step out of the car. The air is fresh and sweet-smelling with the scent of flowers and grass. I watch the car continue to the end of the street until it stops and the lights go out.

I can make out the shadow of my house against the sky. I walk up the steps. The dust grates under my shoes. The door unlocks easily and creaks open. Though it is dark I can find my way. Though the heat of the rooms pricks my skin, I feel comfortable here. One of my relatives has been looking after the house, cleaning it and keeping it ready for my return. I put my suitcase down and lie on the floor.

I sleep. I dream. I am aware of sleep. I am aware of dream. I see myself as a child, then as a boy, then as a man. I see my father. I see my mother. I am conscious it is a dream and therefore I expect nothing from it. No signs of hope or despair. It is a dream that can't help being there, nor can I help it and there is no need to explain or reason it. To wake up and grapple with a dream is to destroy it; then it is no longer a dream but a nightmare.

CHUNI

"Bronson, gimme a light."

Bronson flicked open the lighter and held up the flame. Chuni lit the cigarette, but June Perry and Eileen Veersammy drew his attention.

Chuni muttered between puffs.

"Miss Perry too sweet, like a ripe cherry." Then he chanted, "Morning, Miss Perry!"

"Morning, Chuni."

June Perry spoke lightly, not breaking the rhythm of her progress.

Chuni laughed – a mocking, strangled laugh; then he switched his expression from mirth to hostility, and declared, "These damn women believe they is the Virgin Mary."

Chuni had worked at the university since its founding, when it opened in 1963 and they used to call it 'the communist night school'. Bronson began work only two months ago. Chuni liked to amuse Bronson with his gossip about the staff and students.

The university bus rolled in, stopped before the arts faculty, and deposited a stream of passengers: staff for the administration offices, library, the arts and science faculties, and electricians, carpenters, plumbers. The cleaners queued for the return journey.

The campus was just a year old. From 1963 to 1969, the

university rented buildings in the city, then transferred to this site, a few miles outside the city limits. Young trees, just a few feet high now, would grow tall later. The empty, flat stretches of land between the four main buildings were spread out generously across several acres. The buildings were modestly tall glass and concrete oblongs lying on their sides. Viewed from the East Coast road, they shrank to minute proportions, sandwiched beneath the sky and the table of land. The strong breeze, wind, rain, heat and blinding sunlight had free play here. During the day, it was mostly deserted. The students came at night. They filled up the rooms in the arts and science faculties, and brought to life the sheltered corridors between the faculties, cafeteria, library and registry. The lighting system failed often and plunged whole areas into darkness. The hope was that the campus would eventually house halls of residence, a medical school, and faculties of engineering, law, education and business administration. A university town would bloom, spawn new suburbs along the East Coast, and suck in the city suburbs. New roads would connect the city with the university. Until then, cows grazed on the land and village children sought and found adventure there.

"Look, Lady High-and-Mighty." Chuni pointed to Mrs. Taylor, who was locking up her car.

She was head of the typing pool. Chuni and Bronson were her messengers and machinists. They distributed the university mail, and manned the photocopying and duplicating machines.

"Chuni, Bronson," Mrs. Taylor acknowledged them.

"Morning, Mrs. Taylor," they muttered in unison.

They finished their cigarettes, and Bronson declared, "Chuni, time to work."

Bronson disliked Chuni's thirst for attention, how he stood at the arts faculty each morning and made rude comments about the staff as they arrived. When Bronson first joined the university, Chuni took him under his wing. Bronson was grateful. The pitfalls, as well as the opportunities to make a good impression, were everywhere. Discovering them through experience was hazardous. Enemies could be made, face lost permanently.

They crossed the wide expanse of land between the library and administration offices. They were last to clock in at the typing pool.

Mrs. Taylor commented crisply, "Chuni and Bronson, last as usual."

Half an hour later, Dr. Ambrose visited the typing pool. Chuni was posted behind the duplicator. He was rolling off stencils, turning the handle in a circular, repetitive motion.

"Morning, Doctor!" Chuni greeted him.

Dr. Ambrose smiled, "Morning, Chuni."

Chuni declared loudly, "That is the great doctor himself, the Man, Dr. Ambrose, the greatest lecturer in history ever. The man is a PhD. Look it up in the big Oxford dictionary at the library. It stand for Doctor of Philosophy."

Mrs. Taylor gave Chuni a cutting look before she rose to greet Dr. Ambrose. They shook hands, and sat down at her desk.

Chuni nudged Bronson. "Look, next thing you know, she will lick the man foot-bottom." He raised his voice again, "What you say, Dr. Ambrose?"

Dr. Ambrose turned to glance at Chuni. He murmured patiently, "All right, Chuni, all right."

The typists exchanged looks of disgust. Chuni fixed them with a defiant look.

Mrs. Taylor and Dr. Ambrose settled down, but Chuni continued to interrupt. "Dr. Ambrose, when we having a staff union meeting again?"

Dr. Ambrose turned to Chuni, and replied quickly, "Soon, Chuni, soon."

Mrs. Taylor gave Chuni her most withering look.

"Chuni, Dr. Ambrose and Mrs. Taylor trying to concentrate. Shut up!" Bronson cautioned.

Chuni retorted, "You shut your face."

When Dr. Ambrose was leaving. Chuni called after him, "See you later, Doctor!"

"So long, Chuni," Dr. Ambrose returned, not turning around.

"Nice chap," Chuni continued. "The man been to England, States, Canada, Africa, Germany, Russia. A traveller. Some people been to only one foreign country and come back here as if they come back from heaven. But Dr. Ambrose – unlike them, he travel 'cross the world, meet Malcolm X, Eldridge Cleaver, Stokely Carmichael, President Nyerere of Tanzania. He is socialist, black power, Marxist."

Mrs. Taylor interrupted him wearily, "Chuni, next thing, you're going to enrol as a student in the history department and want to give us real lessons."

Chuni pounced, "And what so strange about that? The university was put here for people like me: the working class, the ordinary people. Nobody don't remember Dr. Jagan say so?"

"Dr. Jagan no longer in power."

"Power?" Chuni retorted. "What is power? It is not something you should use to keep people down. The men who know about real power is men like Fidel Castro, Nyerere, Mao, Che, an' Dr. Jagan and Dr. Ambrose."

"Chuni, come here!" Mrs. Taylor ordered.

"Yes, Mrs. Taylor?"

"Chuni, how many times do I have to tell you not to talk politics in this office? That is one thing. The other thing – I have had to speak with you frequently about being so personal with the staff. Tell me, if everyone always expressing their political views, and taking their eyes and pass the lecturers, abusing them and abusing the students, how will any work get done? We are being paid to run this university smoothly, while the lecturers lecture and the students learn. Chuni, if we are always abusing our function, how will this institution survive? Tell me."

Chuni pondered her questions. "But Mrs. Taylor, I did not take my eyes and pass Dr. Ambrose. I did not say I not here to help run the university. All I do is tell Dr. Ambrose 'Morning'. And I speak my views."

Mrs. Taylor shut her eyes. "Chuni, don't you dare talk down to me. Just don't argue with me." She opened her eyes. "Just don't let me have to speak to you again for the rest of the day. Now go back to your post."

"But, Mrs. Taylor..."

Mrs. Taylor rose quickly, swept up a file, and left the room, straightening her skirt as she went, the file tucked under her arm.

★ ★ ★ ★

One day, Bronson asked Chuni, "You like this job?" It was their lunch break. They were sitting behind the science faculty building, facing the stretch of empty land there.

"Me? If I like this job?"

"Yes. You."

"You see me, if I had my way, I would sit down on my back step whole day minding my birds, man."

Chuni owned a dozen birds, each kept in a separate birdcage, each cage covered by black cloth. On Friday afternoons, he met other bird collectors in an open field near the East Coast railway line. There, the birdmen trained the birds to whistle. Each month, there were competitions to decide the champion whistlers. His birds were the best. It surprised Bronson because Chuni maltreated his birds, pelting their cages with anything not too large or heavy.

He maltreated his wife too. When Bronson visited them, she always stayed out of sight, but once, she appeared on the landing, a white enamel ladle in her right hand, and stared at him for a long time. Irritated, Chuni returned her stare, then told her she looked like the statue of liberty standing there with a pot spoon in her hand. Wordlessly, she retreated back to the kitchen. Since then, whenever Chuni mentioned his wife to Bronson, he called her the statue of liberty.

He enjoyed a reputation as a creator of nicknames. When the staff union sent around a directive asking people to address each other, henceforth, as 'Comrade', it gave him the opportunity to indulge his love of labels. He first saw the directive when he was in the typing pool. He went directly to Mrs. Taylor, held up the pink slip of paper, and asked her, "Comrade, what you think of this?" She did not reply. That day, Chuni found deep satisfaction in addressing everyone as 'Comrade', including the Vice Chancellor.

The campus bloomed with Maoists, Marxists, communists, nationalists, black power advocates, members of the Hindu and Muslim religious societies, the two main political parties and societies for the encouragement of cultural links with India and Africa.

The current government slogan was, *The small man is the real man* and for the last year, the union had fought for the lower grade staff to use the lecturers' common room, and won. Now, instead of sitting behind the science faculty building they began to spend their lunch hour in the lecturers'common room. It was now a union shrine. Human and liquid spirits flowed, but it did not last. The workers drank too much, too often. In the middle of the morning, men turned up drunk for work. Lecturers were driven away by the presence of the workers. For women, the common room became a place of drunkenness and harassment. Numbers dropped until only a hard core of alcoholics and union activists graced the bar. A committee of inquiry reviewed the new arrangement in the common room.

It was through the opening up of the common room that Chuni became infatuated with June Perry. She was Dr. Ambrose's union secretary and when she visited the common room, Chuni displayed his worship in various ways. She listened to his ravings with genuine sympathy.

The Committee of Inquiry frequently summoned Dr. Ambrose and June Perry to give evidence. They drew closer and soon could be seen constantly together on and off the campus.

Chuni's inclinations swung like a pendulum. In his hero-worship he had wedded his spirit to theirs. But their absorption with each other divorced him from their lives. First, he oscillated. Some days he was sure of his old liking for June Perry; some days he was sure he disliked her; some days he was ambivalent and confused, unable to make up his mind. His final solution was to disapprove openly of their relationship. He frequently said, "Miss Perry is a too nice cherry for an old boar like Dr. Ambrose."

One day, the couple were sitting near the bar. Chuni was perched on the barstool. In between gulping down his beer, he shot them cold, hostile looks. Then he claimed the crowd's attention, declaring he wished to disclose that he was writing a thesis. The crowd, ripe and ready, baited him. Someone challenged him to declare the title of his thesis.

"The habits of the boar and the habits of the cherry," he informed them.

His nickname for June Perry was *Perry the Cherry*. Chuni held forth for a long time on the habits of boars and the habit of the cherry. Finally, he concluded, "So I say you can't put new cherry wine in old pigskin bag."

"Nobody can argue with you, Professor Chuni. You do all the research," said Bronson.

"I do all my research yes, field research, behind the science faculty every Wednesday night, ten o' clock sharp."

June Perry and Dr. Ambrose rose as one, and fled the common room. Chuni's strangled laughter chased after them.

After this, Bronson stopped spending his lunch hour with Chuni, stopped going to the cinema and rum shops with him. But, locked in the typing pool with the women, estranged from Chuni, Bronson felt the full force of Mrs. Taylor's authority. When he was sick and requested time off she questioned the truth of his illness. She treble-checked his work. With each passing week, he sank lower in her estimation. He became overeager to please her. She had a repertoire of stock responses, which she kept for those with whom she thought communication impossible or undesirable.

"I finish the job, Mrs. Taylor," from Bronson would be greeted by her with, "I hope so, Bronson, I hope so," and Chuni nicknamed him, *Faith, Hope and Charity*.

Bronson began to try and restore their friendship to its original strength, so when Chuni suggested seeing a film at the Globe Cinema one afternoon, he consented.

There, he found himself sitting in the balcony section, a few rows behind June Perry and Dr. Ambrose. Sitting there near Chuni, Bronson felt his old fear of him return. Bronson went to sleep in the middle of the first film. When the last film was over, Chuni woke him. The lights were coming up, the cinema emptying.

Chuni asked him, "Bronson you want to see something that won't bore you?"

With Chuni on the pillion of his motorcycle, Bronson followed his directions to one of the city's suburbs.

They stopped at a large house. Instead of going to the front gate, Chuni led Bronson to the hedge and before he could speak pushed him through a break.

"Chuni, what the hell is this?" Bronson demanded. "You going to thief or something?"

"Ssh," Chuni cautioned, pointing to the house.

They were standing at the edge of a lawn, behind the house, with the streetlights off, only light from open windows breaking up the darkness. Bronson turned to go, but Chuni held him fast, his hand like a vice round his wrist. Suddenly, footsteps sounded on the outer stairs.

"Duck! Duck!" Chuni whispered, pulling Bronson to the ground.

Low voices accompanied the footsteps. Bronson worked his wrist free from Chuni's grip but stayed where he was, intending to leave as soon as it was clear. The voices murmured on. His eyes became accustomed to the darkness. He made out the cesspit a few yards away. His eyes ached, his body was stiff with tension. Now, the voices ceased and footsteps sounded, coming towards them. Then the footsteps ceased and the voices began again, closer this time – a man and woman. Then Bronson saw them. They were vague shapes in the darkness, outlined against the trellis wall. The two shapes merged and became one. The couple's breathing, Chuni's, his own, were like the ticking of separate clocks, each keeping a different time, sounding separate notes.

Bronson turned to Chuni, "Chuni, you damn Peeping Tom!" He sucked his teeth and stood up.

He disturbed the couple. Their noises ceased abruptly.

They must have seen him for the woman's voice cried out, "Oh Lord!"

Bronson recognised June Perry's voice. Then the man shouted angrily, "Who's there? Who's there? Who's there?" It was Dr. Ambrose.

"Chuni you madman!" Bronson screamed, echoing Dr. Ambrose's outrage, and he began to kick Chuni where he lay on the ground. He kicked wildly, struck blindly.

Chuni's voice seemed to come from far away, pleading with him.

Bronson could not hear. In the rage of his own injury, breath seemed to come only from within his own body. It fed his lungs, heart and flesh. The more he struck the louder the noise grew. When the strength in his feet failed he sat on Chuni and pummelled him with his fists. When the strength in his arms failed he dropped exhausted beside Chuni. The throbbing in his head slowed, then stopped. Lying on his back Bronson saw the sky. Above the dark night it was a thin blue skin wrapped over the flesh of the earth.

VERA

This time of morning, Bel Air quiet as an empty country church. The Vincent girlchild still there on the veranda, so soon in the morning, by herself, for all to see, only in her nightie. Where her mother, Mrs. Vincent? None of my business, but the sink so near the window, you have to look outside the same time as you do the washing.

Six o' clock and the Vincent girlchild still there in her nightie, in broad daylight. Better worry about your own child. Pray to God Susan remember to get to the standpipe by six o' clock or else after six o' clock the whole village wanting water same time. Six o' clock the estate turn on the water supply. Eight o' clock they turn it off again. Midday next day they turn it on again. Two o'clock they turn it off again. Pray to God she remember to clean the house, sweep the yard, and look after Winston and Marcus.

You do the best to discipline children. When you not there it in God hands what become of them. Better to work in Plaisance if you could get the work, but Plaisance has no work. Georgetown has all the work.

The whole of last year the work was with the merchants in Water Street. The job was picking out rotten onions, potatoes and garlic and selling what you keep. You had to walk up and down in the hot sun whole day. This job with

Mrs. Semple is better. Bel Air is a clean place. The maid uniform save on clothes-spending and nobody to overseer you whole day and you have the whole quiet and peaceful house to yourself – although Mrs. Semple like to make plenty work to keep you busy. That hot sun, that walking up and down Water Street, the begging people to buy is terrible.

Seven o' clock – Mrs. Semple soon to open the kitchen door. The Vincent girlchild still on the veranda. The mother must be ill to let her stand outside in her nightgown like that.

The sink and washing machine want cleaning, the floor want wiping, and then when that finish, put on the maid-uniform.

The Vincent girlchild still there – and nearly a young woman, her hair not even comb, just the scarf round her head, maybe not even bathe yet.

The Semples wake up now. All talking. Footsteps, shower running, voices. At last, Mrs Semple open the kitchen door, and want breakfast to start right away.

"Morning, Vera."

"Morning, ma'am."

Bacon and eggs to cook, toast to toast, coffee to make.

Eight o' clock. Front gates opening, cars starting. Rush hour time in Georgetown. Schoolchildren, office people, cycling to town. Not Mrs.Semple. No orders for the day till she finish all her showering and dressing – after eleven – then only coffee for her. No eating for her till lunchtime – the diet – then she will go to work at her father, at his insurance office, Main Street.

"Vera, you see the Vincent child on the veranda?"

Say no. Just take the kitchen mat outside, shake it, come back in and say nothing.

"Vera, the electrician is coming to fix the fridge today. Make sure it is working before he goes away."

"Yes, ma'am."

"Look, here's fifteen dollars on the kitchen table. Don't spend it all. We need fresh fruit in the house. If no prawns, get some fish at the market. Whatever, clean and salt and freeze it. I can't stand the supermarket fish. It taste like paper."

"Yes, ma'am."

"Why is that child on the veranda? The car is not under the house either."

Outside: get vacuum cleaner; upstairs: tidy, clean, air and make beds, dust and vacuum; downstairs again: sweep yard.

When Mr. Vincent driving, you hear the big fancy car before you see it. Mrs. Semple always talking about Mr. Vincent and his car. And when you finally see him in it, the car so big he has it right up to the gate. And he call call call until the maid or gardener or his daughter come and open for him. But now he jump out himself and open the gate, and the whole street can hear him calling his girlchild, "Margaret, go inside!" I never hear him run up the front steps so fast and slam the door so hard.

Mrs. Semple crane her neck to see better and ask, "Vera, you see Mr. Vincent come in? I haven't seen Mrs. Vincent this morning. I wonder if she gone to the university yet? Why is Mr. Vincent in such a big hurry?"

Now she will stay at home and wait to find out, no matter how long. No bed-making, no hoovering until she finish playing with all her clothes in the wardrobe and the make-up in the vanity.

"Vera, switch off that Hoover! Do the downstairs first. I can't stand that noise. Wait until I leave."

"Yes, ma'am."

"I'll get the telephone; Vera, you dust the vanity. I'm finished there."

"Yes, ma'am."

"Gordon?"

Mr. Vincent is Gordon.

"Oh my god, Gordon, I am so so sorry, so sorry, my good heavens! But I saw Margaret on the veranda and I felt in my bones unconsciously... Yes, all right. Yes. I will come over. Right away. I must phone and tell Harry. Right away. I'll be over. Vera!"

"Yes, ma'am?"

"Stop what you are doing. We have to go over to the Vincents. Mrs. Vincent died this morning. I have to ring Harry and tell him."

Mr. Semple is Harry.

"Harry, you would never believe this. Hilda has died. Yes. Gordon just telephoned to tell me. Look, I am going over this instant. I don't know. I don't know the details. God, man, I hear just this second, this instant, this moment. I am going over. I knew something was up. Yes, all right. Call him. OK."

"Mrs. Semple, how Mrs. Vincent could die so?"

"Vera, don't ask questions. Come along. Vera, don't just stand there, man. Lock the back door. Shut the windows. We will have to forget about the electrician. He will just have to come back another time. The fridge will have to wait. God have mercy on us. Out of the blue. Out of the blue. I saw the woman coming in from university only yesterday. I didn't know she was ill."

Mrs. Vincent can't die. She too young. She originally from the country, from Plaisance, from *your part of the world* she use to tell me. Twice, Mrs. Vincent bake a cake, and three times give a cardboard box full with clothes for the children; and school books, pens, and soursop and mangoes from her yard; and always ask, "How is Susan doing at school? And Winston? Marcus?" I never refuse from her anything but I always keep a distance. I always answer her inquiries but make sure never to expect anything. Never mind Mrs. Vincent come from the country too, there is age to consider. Mrs. Vincent is thirty-seven years old, fifteen years younger. Mrs. Vincent is such a beautiful woman. Mr. Vincent and the two children are a credit to her. How come she could die so?

"Mistress, Mrs. Vincent dead?"

"Yes, Vera, you heard me. For God's sake, Vera! Don't stand like a statue with your mouth hanging open. Come along, man!"

Mrs. Semple stepping into Mrs. Vincent house like the owner.

"Come through, Vera, come through. What is the matter with you? What are you doing?"

"Taking off my shoes, ma'am."

"What for? Vera, put your shoes on. No one told you to take off your sandals. What is the matter with you?"

"I didn't want to dirty the floor, ma'am."

"Well wipe your feet on the mat. Come with me. Let us go and hear what Mr. Vincent needs doing in the house. Come along."

It is good they keep open the sliding door to let in the breeze but too much sunlight falling on the floor will damage the polish.

"Vera, make coffee."

In the kitchen, Mrs. Vincent handbag still right on the dresser where she leave it. A leather one, good and used. I always see Mrs. Vincent with it round her shoulder, never without it – coming and going to work, coming and going from the supermarket and market.

Why the girlchild follow me to the kitchen? To check on me?

"Vera, look here in the cupboards for the cups."

"Yes, ma'am."

Now Mrs Semple come in the kitchen too to keep an eye on me. Now she holding the girlchild as if it is her own child.

"Margaret, go and change out of your nightie."

"I'm all right, Mrs. Semple."

"Go on, people will be coming soon."

"Oh, all right."

"You have everything in your room?"

"Yes."

"Vera, you had better make a large pot of coffee. The doctor is here."

"Yes, ma'am"

Footsteps coming up the front stairs. The doorbell ringing and ringing and more and more voices in the house. Back and forth, Mrs. Semple is coming and going, like the mistress, and ordering more and more coffee, wasting it.

Now Mrs. Carew come; she and Mrs. Vincent teach at the university. She is the first one I see crying, eyes red red, and saying, "Vera, look what befall us."

Mrs. Carew help me serve the coffee. Mrs. Semple would never help me serve the coffee. Mrs. Carew always used to give Mrs. Vincent lifts; they always chatting in the car a long time, always waving at each other until the car drive away. If Mrs. Carew pass me on the street in her car, she always stop and say, "Come Vera, I will give you a lift." Mrs. Carew just like Mrs. Vincent, friendly, chatty, bright.

★ ★ ★ ★

This kitchen like a graveyard, and me like a jumbie waiting and waiting. Please God, let me outside on the landing, let me me sit down out here and rest my bones. This breeze is merciful. But look, Mrs. Vincent bedroom window still open. Nobody think to shut it? All the light of day and the breeze pouring in through the open window over Mrs. Vincent's corpse.

"Lord, Lord!"

"What is it, Vera? What is it?"

"God, Mrs. Carew. Oh Lord, ma'am, oh Lord! Mrs. Vincent was so kind to me! She was such a young woman to die!"

"All right, Vera, all right. You don't have to cry so hard. Don't make so much noise, Vera. Please calm down, you will fall down if you don't stop shaking."

"Oh, Mrs. Semple, Mrs. Semple, Mrs. Vincent dead dead dead!"

"Vera! Let go of Mrs. Carew at once! Behave yourself! Stop this disgusting noise at once! Do you hear me?"

Lord, make me stop the grieving or they will take away my job.

"I sorry, Mrs. Semple."

"Vera, honestly! Do you think you are at a wake?"

"Vera, Mrs. Semple, I think we should put away Hilda's things now, before the undertaker arrives."

"Yes, Mrs. Carew, yes, Mrs. Semple."

"Gordon says he can't face it. There's her jewellery. We should make sure it's safely locked away. Vera, you come with us. Collect the laundry from the bathroom. Take it over to our place for washing."

"Yes, Mrs. Semple."

Look how Mrs. Vincent corpse straight straight straight like a rod. My people say, always show respect for the dead, speak to them, ask them to send you a blessing. Mrs. Carew and Mrs. Semple not speaking, they just walking about her room, handling her clothes and jewellery, and showing no respect at all.

I must speak.

"Mrs. Vincent, I ask you to blow a good breeze on me and my family, ma'am. I begging you to blow a very good breeze on us."

PART TWO

HOPSCOTCH

1974

Each morning a bottle of milk appears at the front door, like a gift. The milkman comes and goes without a word, as silent as the draught pouring through the sliver of a gap under the front door. Milk and draught concentrate into one idea: hot sun, melting ice cream, Carmen, Dell and everyone like bees swarming round the ice cream churn.

"My turn! My turn!"

"Salt the ice! Turn the churn!"

The ice is grating and breaking and crushing between the wooden tub and metal urn.

"Keep it freezing!"

Turning, taking turns, racing to be first to eat the cold ice cream with the fresh nutmeg and vanilla.

"Who turn the most?"

"Me, me, I turn the most!"

"No Carmen, not you. Sylvia turn the most. Give Sylvia the biggest glass of ice cream!"

Cold was the luxury. Solid ice cream chewed and swallowed like food, drinks filled to the rim, ice-cold glasses to cool hot hands, ice chewed to chill and numb your teeth and tongue, to cool the sun.

Dear Sylvia,

I don't know why you want to go and live in a cold country like England. That is all it is, cold, cold, cold. And regimented, rainy, damp and grey. They do not respect family or friendship there. Come back home.

Carmen

Dear Carmen,

You know very well why I had to leave Guyana. Burnham's thugs were trying to kill us. Every night, they used to stone all the houses in the street because a few of the lecturers who supported Walter Rodney lived there. Guyana has also destroyed its people's lives and turned friends and family against each other.

Sylvia

Dear Sylvia,

Things will get better. You cannot write off your own people, your own country. Come back home. You say yourself you are not happy in England, so why are you living there?

Carmen

In England, heat is the luxury. In the dark of the winter morning, he vacates his side of the bed and the cocoon of heat shrinks to a tiny envelope of warmth. There is a trick to sleeping without him: don't move or else cold air pockets get in.

A cold body is a dead body. When you die, you die feet first.

Don't go pelting downstairs without a warm dressing gown or else you turn to ice as soon as your feet touch the carpet. Cold is the air you breathe. Cold is the damp in your clothes. Cold is the sweat on your skin. London is not a place for eating ice cream. It doesn't just cool you down; it chills you to the bone, to the heart. Strange to drink the cold milk and not know where or who it belongs to. At home, they bring the warm milk from the farms in the forest straight after milking, on a cart full of big churns. The farmer will stop at each cottage in the village and ladle the warm milk into pots held up by ragged children like me. Now I am drinking strange milk, in the strange cold, in a strange kitchen with red floor tiles and white wall tiles.

Warming the milk on the gas stove, it is still white as the cold snow outside. Cold white snow on the earth as smooth as ice cream.

The editor here struck out 'white snow' from my manuscript but left in 'hot sun'. She said, " *White* snow is stating the obvious."

"But not *hot* sun?"

"No," she said.

Dear Sylvia,
That is cultural imperialism....

Dear Dell,
No, it is failure to appreciate the difference...

Dear Sylvia,
How can you say that. These people are publishers...

Dear Dell,
You exaggerate their importance...

I am a child taking the milk pot to the stove for boiling. In the afternoon, when the milk cools and a film of cream forms, I spoon off the cream and eat it with some of the black sugar they throw away at the sugar factory. No one in Guyana likes to eat black sugar. They prefer the expensive, pure white granulated sugar when it comes back from England with all the molasses removed. They call brown sugar Demerara Sugar, but it comes from sugar estates in Berbice. There is only one sugar factory in Demerara: Diamond Estate.

Boil the English milk with the white sugar that is so cheap here. When it is cool and the film of cream forms, eat it and hope it tastes right. But no, there is always hardly any cream; it is always watery and stale. It doesn't matter. You are lucky milk is brought to your door. Lucky to have any food at all to eat. In Guyana, there are bad food shortages. Remember the food queues. Remember the lecturers they shoot, beat, stone and kidnap. In 1971 the government was begging educated nationals to return from overseas and build Guyana. After three years, they were chasing them from the country. Remember the men in the Volkswagens who came at night to stone us for criticising the government. Some of my old friends sent them.

Dear Sylvia,

Tell them in England not to keep giving us such a bad press. They can never write anything good about us. Don't be one of those writers in exile who can only bad talk your own people, your own country.

Dell

Dear Dell,

They were kidnapping and shooting lecturers at the university. A stone fell near Sammy's cot. I don't want to work or raise my child in Guyana. The government deserves a bad press if it kills people. Don't call me an exile. I chose to come here. I am not an exile.

Sylvia

The letters from home come through the gap under the door with the draught.

1990

This is the first warm and sunny day of the year in London. Days like this open memory like a book. There is no more snow, no more Gulf war.

The phone is ringing like an alien thing, like an aeroplane or a motorboat to people in the bush – a machine that has nothing to do with them. But it would not go away, not like a plane or motorboat.

"Hello?"

"Sylvia, I thought you mightn't be there. You took a long time to answer!"

"I was half-asleep."

"I thought you would like to know that your good friend Carmen is here from Guyana."

"Carmen? Here?"

"At International House."

"I will phone her straight away. Thanks for telling me."

"You and Carmen were always good friends. I thought I should tell you. One of my relatives came in from Guyana on the same plane with her, two weeks ago. I think she is leaving in a couple of days so you have to be quick if you want to catch her."

"I had a letter from her two weeks ago. She said nothing about coming to England."

The switchboard operator says 'Carmen' with her English voice. So comforting the sound of her name, even on English lips. It is the sound of two worlds coming together, an English voice pronouncing the name of an old friend from Guyana.

"Hello?"

"Carmen?"

"Yes?"

"Sylvia here."

"Sylvia! Sylvia! Oh but this is great! How come you knew I was here?"

"Susan Harris phoned to tell me. She said a relative of hers came in on the same plane with you."

"Lord, wherever Guyanese go, news travels so fast with them! I never got to tell you I was coming. It happened too fast. Anyway, when I'll see you?"

"Right away if you want."

"No no, come tomorrow after work. You are working?"

"I have some time off due. I will come anytime you want."

"You mean to say you will take time off for me?"

"Of course. We go back a long way, Carmen, childhood."

"No, don't do that. I have a busy schedule, plenty of research to finish; I am going home in two days."

"What about first thing in the morning, nine o' clock, before you start?"

"Good, that is good. See you at nine then."

At International House, the porter phones Carmen to come down, then he stays around to observe us and this makes her mad.

"I have to expect this. It is England. It is white people's country. After all we are only guests in this country!"

Still, she demands a real English breakfast.

"You must know where to get one now you've been living here so long. Take me on a bus, a red and double-decker English bus, then show me Soho."

Outside the building, away from the prying porter, Carmen is not ashamed to say she wants to be a tourist. There is a cafe off Charing Cross Road, a bus ride away. She used to swear she could never leave Guyana to live in 'white people country'. Now she is lapping up London's sights and sensations.

All the way it is just talk talk talk non-stop – about

everyone we went to school with, who lived where and was doing what.

"Girl, you are looking so good. How many years we haven't seen each other?"

"Too many."

"Too right!"

There are few friendships like this to bring back my girlhood, to make me remember the taste of food I never eat any more; to make me remember the feel of Guyana sun and rain and breeze; to make me remember walking barefoot on a hand-polished floorboard; sleeping under a mosquito net, and going to the market. She makes me feel as if I could be completely my same old self.

"Why you so quiet, man? Don't be so English."

"Nothing to do with being English."

"Well, to me that is really English."

"Don't call me English."

"The trouble with you is you forget what it is to be yourself. You are English now. English, English, English."

"Carmen, if anything makes me forget how to be myself, how to be with you, it is what happened in Guyana, and you are part of that corrupt government that destroyed it."

"I have told you I will not listen to you criticising your country. It is that Englishman you married who has turned you against us."

"It is not him. He helped me to escape from it. You tell me to speak my feelings, and when I speak them, you attack me. You don't want me to speak. You are afraid to let me speak."

"That is not true. I am going now."

"I am talking but you don't want to hear what I am saying."

1993

The thatch on the cottages here could just as well be thatch on a benab. Suffolk is flat like Guyana. In Devon, there is a small town called Westward Ho, a ridiculous name, but there is a seawall there, a real seawall that looks just like the Georgetown seawall. Even the benches are similar. Sometimes, England can be like Guyana.

Dell's face is at the window of the thatched cottage. Her energetic voice is out of place in this understated English place. She jumps out of the door with excitement. Twenty-one years difference in time, but no difference in person.

"I was expecting you since eleven!"

"The traffic was too terrible. I can't tell you!"

We take the deckchairs outside for the English ritual of sitting out to have tea in the summer, in an English country garden. The grass is parched the colour of the thatch by this long, dry, global-warming summer.

"You got a good summer for finishing your thesis, Dell."

"Thank god. Last year I was here in the summer, it was like winter to me."

"My first winter here was hell. They say winters here will be getting warm now and islands will disappear. They say it will happen at home. You think there is anything in it? Can you see Barbados, Jamaica, Cuba, Haiti all sinking in the Caribbean Sea?"

"Don't go telling island people that. They will say you are showing off because you are Guyanese and don't have no island to sink."

"You cook so much food."

"Look, just relax. You are the guest. Rest."

We drink the hot tea quickly, like cold drinks, then Dell brings out plates of steaming hot prawn curry, and we lie on the ground at four, in the English afternoon, and eat the curry like guests at a wedding. In between conversation, the quiet of the village frames itself like a soundbox round our voices. But it was more than the village. It was Dell and all the memories of our lives falling out of the big, blue summer sky that is like the Guyana sky.

"Drink, drink."

"I don't drink, Dell."

"Well this is a celebration, so just drink. Just relax and eat and drink. You see me here. I worked hard for twenty years and I tell myself – now I am not worrying about a thing. Relax up yourself, woman."

"You come to live here now? Your professor will find you a job?"

"I am only a guest in foreign. I would not live here. I am settled in Trinidad, until they throw me out."

"You ran away to Trinidad. I ran away to London but I can't think in London."

"You mean all this time you live here you never think?"

"Very funny, Dell. You going to give me a hard time too for living in London, like Carmen has done all these years? I will never go home because Guyana has changed for the worst, because we have all changed and we are different now, too different."

"You changed! Because you came to live in England. You could have stayed in the Caribbean. Why you had to go so far away?"

"Tell me why I should have stayed?"

"We Guyanese all want to escape from Guyana. We hate the ones who get out because we really want to get out too."

"You and Carmen worked with Burnham. Those are the things that made us change, not me marrying an Englishman, not me leaving Guyana to live here. I have lived here with too much grief for England to impress me. I live with Guyana all the time. I want to stop my memory, stop remembering, so I can start to live here."

"Lord, I don't want to argue about it. Please don't let us talk politics."

"There is politics between us women too."

"Don't start with that."

"Why, why not? Why did Carmen have to try so hard for so many years to break up my marriage?"

"Carmen is against marriage, not your husband. Don't forget Anna made us into feminists. She brought it with her from Paris."

Anna came to us in the same year the army came in warships on a rare high tide, when muddy harbours turned traitor. Fathers and brothers massed for defence, prepared to die for politics. We learned to ride bicycles through the strikes and riots. There was a drought followed by a downpour and that was the finish of grandmother's garden, ducks and chickens. Never again to wake to collect new laid eggs warm from the womb of hens. When Anna came to our school, we were ripe for love. She took us to her house and gave us English tea and biscuits. Dell and her talk of memories is warming, filling and sensuous as the hot, sweet, freshly baked coconut buns of childhood, eaten as soon as they were fished from the huge, wood-fired oven with a large wooden paddle. Buns so hot and delicious, you could let your fingers burn holding them to your lips while you blow on the open halves to cool them. Eating the bun quickly, you ate your own breath, the power of lungs and tongue and speech. Uncle Stephen made the buns. Uncle Stephen who courted Aunt Martha so well, for us to see. Love, hot buns and Caribbean tongue. So much pain and pleasure, it is hard to distinguish between them, between friend and enemy. The memories are so strong now because Dell is making them strong. I have to remind myself we are in a cottage at the roadside of a solitary part of the English countryside. We are in England. I am living in the past. Dell too. Although she is here, thinking and writing far away from Guyana, being together turns it into a natural soundbox of memory. Even the silence of an English village can resonate with Guyanese history.

"Dell, I have seen Cuba open and shut, and open again."

"Yes, Russia is opening."

"After all these years."

"1963 Russia was very closed."

"In 1963, there was a bookshop in Georgetown where they sold the works of Karl Marx and Lenin. It used to be Red House Bookshop, then Michael Forde Bookshop when a bomb killed Michael Forde. I was beginning to read those books then. Guyana was going to become communist, another Cuba. I was educating myself for it. I think of those books as stained with blood now. People died for that. Guyana was going to become the first English-speaking Communist country in the whole world."

"That was not my scene. It was yours."

"But Dell, you and Carmen went into politics too, but we were on opposite sides. Now you are doing your thesis on Caribbean poetry and Derek Walcott is going to be reading in London with Joseph Brodsky. They say Walcott is going to win the Nobel Prize soon, too. A Caribbean and Russian writer reading together and not a whiff of Communism in it. Everything full circle."

"Those things, all the politics, it still means a lot to you?"

"Yes."

"But it is outdated. All that gone. It is history. It is full of blood and killing, broken dreams, broken friendships, broken lives."

"Now the bookshops in London are selling Russian books. It's all right to read Russian books again."

"Life is crazy. I am sorry Carmen was not nice. Carmen is very in with the government."

"In 1990, when she came to London, she did not want to see me, because I was still on the government black list. She did not like me having old memories. I was not sure we were still friends. Yet all these years, because I had no way of knowing what she had become, I kept her in my heart as a childhood friend. If I had stayed in Guyana we would have been enemies."

"Don't say that. Our mothers were friends. We must always respect that. You live in England too long. People are so individualistic here, they give up families and friends and community without a care. That is what you are trying to do with Carmen. Give her up."

"But Carmen gave me up. In her politics, she gave us up. Carmen is powerful in Guyana. That is why you are afraid to criticise her. It was the same with Anna. She was so colonial in her mentality, so arrogant."

"Don't talk like this. You are too English now. You are rejecting everything you are."

"No, I am trying to be who I am, to grow out of Anna and Carmen. I am always trying to grow out of them. Do you remember the year Anna came to our school?"

"1962. Russia was shut then."

"Cuba was open."

The food, drink, heat, the pleasure of Dell's company, the rush of memories, the drone of the tractor – all combine into one drug: the past.

When Dell makes tea, she has to use her hostess's English Earl Grey tea kept in a simulated Chinese tin, in Wedgwood cups, using Sheffield silver cutlery. She handles the tea-making ritual like a borrower taking library books to the counter to be issued. Like borrowed books from the British Council library in old Georgetown in British Guiana so many moons ago, books borrowed by schoolgirls more than twenty years ago. Too long ago for memory. These memories have nowhere to go, only here, England, 1993. Memory turns the years into a vicious circle and attacks the present. Dell is still like a girl. We are still girls with each other. I become a girl again with them. That is what happened when Carmen came. We had one of our childish arguments, as if we were not forty, but fifteen. We will never grow up. Like our country.

In bed, memory becomes a soundbox again. Anna's voice enters it.

Bonjour mes amis.

No teacher ever called a pupil 'friend', not in English, not in any other language, and not in our own language, not the Creole we were not permitted to speak. She overstepped the mark when she seduced us all.

"Voila!" She wrote her name on the blackboard with pride.

"Voici. Here are your books."

"Fait. Take them."

"Levez-vous! Stand up."

"Asseyez-vous! Sit down."

Every word she spoke was understood even before she uttered it. A romance language. Anna in Paris at the Sorbonne, then Anna in British Guiana, then Guyana. The city in the village. The village in the city. Black faces, white masks. White faces, black masks. Anna knew about Fanon before it was fashionable to know about Fanon in the English-speaking Caribbean. That, she said, was because the French-speaking Caribbean was ahead in intellectual ideas.

"Mademoiselle! Comment appellez-vous?"

"Je m'appelle Sylvia."

"Très bien, Mademoiselle. Merci. Asseyez-vous."

"Merci."

Anna was the most perfect woman in the world. She came to teach us when we were young and as expectant as arrivals in a new country. Anna, living to make us scholars and writers. She joined the People's National Congress. They say that when she did national service, she broke down and wept at having to clean chicken coops. They say she worshipped Forbes Burnham and he was the father she never had. How she betrayed herself, how she betrayed us!

Uncle Stephen was the most perfect man in the world. He built a house, and a car. Kites flew because of him. Perhaps Aunt Martha, not Anna, was really the most perfect woman. Aunt Martha had to be the one because she was married to Uncle Stephen.

> *Dear Sylvia,*
>
> *This is your Aunt Mary, your Aunt Martha's sister, writing to let you know Martha has had a stroke and she is now paralysed on one side and lost her speech. I am also sorry to tell you that their eldest son, Terrence, has killed himself. He left a note to say that he cannot live with the memory of how his father terrorised him and the whole family.*
>
> *Love, Aunt Mary*

One week, the skies opened and sent a flood. The house almost drowned with all of us. It washed away Grandmother's garden. It had taken three years of her life to grow. Her chickens and ducks died. No biblical flood, just New Testament Christianity. No garden for us, just the sin of losing faith and you must hide it so well even you cannot find it, until the circle ends so that it festers away in darkness until it matures into a ripe evil. Uncle Stephen lives in Australia now. Aunt Martha wanted the perfect man, the perfect marriage, and the perfect family.

"Sylvia, Sylvia, wake up."

"I was dreaming."

OH BUDDHA

She didn't know what to expect but it was disappointing to see that the Clinic in Cricklewood was really just an ordinary house, not all that nice. It needed a good coat of paint and the plants outside didn't look healthy either.

The woman who opened the door looked Italian or Greek, like Mrs Romani in Ridley Road. All this time, she'd been expecting an Englishwoman because her voice was so posh on the phone.

"Hello," she said. "Come in." Her voice sounded friendlier but her face was serious.

The carpet and the wallpaper in the hall needed changing. Business couldn't be that good.

"Take off your coat and leave it here. Take off your shoes too, then come into the front room. We've started."

She pointed to the back of the hall. It was full of coats thrown across the chairs and desk, and boots and shoes on the floor. Why did they have to take off their shoes? And why, with so many people here, the place so quiet?

She took off her coat and shoes and followed the therapist into the front room where only women, no men, were sitting in a circle on the floor.

"I don't know if I can manage to sit on the floor."

The therapist frowned and her friendly face changed quickly into an angry face, then changed back quickly again into a smiling face. " You can bring one of the chairs in."

But now she didn't want to be the odd one out so she said,

"It's okay. I'll try out the floor, only I'm not used to it. It makes me feel like a small child again."

The therapist smiled a different kind of smile, a knowing smile. The way she had of changing her voice and her facial expressions, one after another, was really disturbing.

All the women were young.

"We're just doing our round, introducing ourselves," the therapist explained, then smiled and nodded at one of the women.

This woman said, "I'm Margaret. I've come a long way tonight, from Hackney. On the way here I felt very nervous about starting group therapy. I almost turned back because I was so nervous, and I'm still feeling really nervous. I want to be in therapy to try and sort myself out. I am thirty-three and I still can't get on with my mother. She really really upsets me and I felt it was time I did something about it. So I hope you can help."

"Thank you, Margaret," the therapist said.

The three women who spoke after Margaret talked about their problems. They all talked about trouble with their parents and their relationships with their partners and their worries about getting support in the group. By the time it came to her turn she was feeling very frightened – and annoyed with herself for being frightened. After all, they were all women together and that was the time when you could talk freely about men and problems with them. That was why she came here, to talk about Charley and get some help sorting him out. He was getting so crotchety, with his head balding, and his paunch getting bigger and this and that fretting him and making her life miserable.

She found herself saying all this, not using words like relationship and partner like the other women, just talking about Charley. She couldn't stop talking once she started until the therapist said:

"I have to stop you."

After this, the therapist made them play a game. They had to take turns at being blindfolded and led around the flat by a partner. They had to choose this partner by instinct, by looking at each other. If the other person nodded, that was the sign that she wanted to be your partner. This choosing took a long time. She was going to wait for someone to choose her but got fed up and just nodded when she felt like it and the other woman nodded back, so they started before everyone else. The blindfolded person had to learn to trust her partner to lead her round the room, giving her various objects to touch and handle, let her feed her bits of food the therapist had left lying around. She had no trouble with this game, she didn't feel afraid or nervous as the therapist suggested they might feel. But she felt fed up with it because all she wanted to do was talk about Charley and get some advice about sorting him out.

After this, they had to do a feedback round, with everyone saying how they felt doing the trust exercise. When it came to her turn, she said she found it boring and just wanted to get on with getting some advice about dealing with Charley. She said, too, that *she* did not have trouble with her mother. In fact, she wished her mother were here instead of in Guyana because she would sort out Charley for her.

When this round was over, the therapist made a little speech. She talked about how difficult women found it to make time for themselves, how guilty they felt about it, how they were used to giving and not receiving, how hard they found it to be assertive. She said that their time here with her was time just for them to learn to use, to get what they needed, to empower them. She said it was important for everyone to feel able to have trust in the group. There were rules: no violence, no drugs and no sex in the group. Then she said they had to finish in ten minutes but could use the time left doing a final round, and this she called the resentment round. She wanted everyone to express any resentment they experienced during the session. The therapist asked her to start and she said she felt the hour had been a disappointment because she came for some advice about how to handle Charley and didn't get it, so she was going home feeling disappointed.

The other women had no resentment but when it came to the therapist's turn, she looked straight at her and put on her angry face. She said to her, " I felt very resentful of you for several reasons. You have done nothing but complain throughout the session, about having to sit on the floor at the start, but mainly you were continually having a power struggle with me. I also resented you touching Margaret because she was crying. You were invading her space..."

She felt herself getting very angry. "I only touch her to comfort her. Don't talk nonsense to me for God's sake..."

One of the other women, Carol, put her hand up and said she wanted to express resentment after all. The therapist gave her permission. Carol said, "I am a Christian and I resent you, for taking God's name in vain. I don't feel I can be in a group with someone who does not respect God."

"Oh God! " she cried out, totally fed up, and got up to leave. "I didn't know this was a church group, if I want to be in a church group, I would go to church. And let me tell you, when I say 'Oh God' it is not a sign of disrespect, I am asking God for help!"

The therapist was smiling now and this was making her feel really angry.

"Anyway, I won't be coming back here since I am not wanted."

Now the therapist put on her kind face. " Please don't go, we do want you here. Sit down and let us work through the fear of rejection and anger you brought here with you. Maybe you need a round for yourself? Why don't you go round and ask everyone how they feel about having you here?"

"What for? This one, Carol, said she didn't want me because I call on God."

Carol complained, "You were abusing God. When you say 'Oh God', you are abusing God."

The therapist, still smiling, said, "I tell you what, let's sort it out this way. Let's agree not to say 'Oh God!' but 'Oh Buddha!' instead, then nobody can be offended.

She put on her coat but the therapist followed her and asked her to return and work on her anger with the group.

"You work on your own anger," she said, and left.

THE GODMOTHER

"Put it in her palm, then she will always have luck."

I did it, just as Mother said, and like magic or luck, the baby opened her palm and took the coin. Then they took it from her and put it with the rest of her money and presents.

★ ★ ★ ★

Now her father was telephoning. His voice was travelling not just through the telephone line but also in my memory. Outside, the English rain is falling. People are passing by but I can still see his face: jovial, happy. A tall, strong, handsome man for a child to idealise.

Am I making him up? Did I use to make him up? He is speaking my name with an accent and intonation that is not a Georgetown voice, not a New Amsterdam voice, but a Canje voice, the one that was too familiar to be mistaken for any other a mile or ten or twenty or seventy or a hundred miles upriver or up the road. He is sounding just like my father, many years dead now and buried where I was born.

When she expected a visit from a special visitor, my mother used to enact laborious rituals of cleansing and cooking. I was witness to this ritual for so many years that

I also perfected it. I dust the entire house: ceilings, walls, books, shelves, furniture, wash all the dust away with soap and water then rinse with perfumed water. If we'd had carpets they would have been shampooed, so I shampoo the carpets. The labour of preparation never wearied my mother; it charged her with energy. I still mimic this behaviour, her preparation for receiving people, not just cleaning and cooking, but making something extraordinary happen.

I plan Guyanese food for my long-lost godchild and her parents: calaloo-and-egg soup, pepperpot, ground provisions, salt-fish and boiled eggs in a wash of olive oil with fried onions and tomatoes, fried ochroes, chicken curry and roti, hassa cooked in coconut and rice, chow mien, black cake. From their hiding places, I take precious casareep, rum and cassava bread smuggled into London. Like Mother, I will take out my best china and glasses for these guests. In cooking this meal, perhaps a dream will come true.

I have to travel across London, to Brixton, to buy sorrel, soursop, hassa, mangoes, papaya, wiri-wiri, and ball-of-fire pepper. The journey is familiar. I can close my eyes and find my way round the underground. Usually I check the route on the underground map at the platform while I wait for the train. Sitting in the carriage I read the smaller replica of the same map on the ceiling of the carriage and count the stops when the train pulls in and out of stations. Today I ignore these maps.

Today, my feet, not my eyes and Brixton landmarks, take me to the market. I don't stop in at the Ritzy for a programme or phone Claudia to see if she is in. I don't stay all day shopping in the market with her and eating lunch. I don't visit Cecil's Bakery for salara and pine tarts. I go straight to Evan's and he gives me the sorrel and soursop he says just came from Trinidad and he tells me I am lucky to get the wiri-wiri and thick-leaf thyme from Guyana because he is growing it himself in his own kitchen. The return journey is the same – no maps.

In winter, the kitchen is the coldest room in the house. The draught pours though the door, along the tiled floor, snaps at my heels, and gnaws at my feet. But I am in another world as I cook. In that world, the sun is hot. Naturally, my god-daughter's christening was on a Sunday, at midday.

Sunday was a family day. We would all be together at home, living in slow time with the newspapers to read and lunch to cook and eat at leisure. It is the one day Father and Mother sleep in the afternoon. They sleep outdoors in the hammocks under the mango trees. This memory is very easy to live. I slide into it so easily, like a contented child going to sleep between clean sheets fresh from drying in the sun and fresh air. Sometimes, it is this easy to live in the past and present.

Happy, I begin to peel the onions, boil the water and heat the oil. The clock reminds me I have three hours to cook the meal before the Allens are here. When he telephoned, I could not remember their names. He was Joseph, his wife was Cynthia, and my goddaughter was Yvette. Now their faces in my mind have their rightful names. This brings with it the placing of people to places. The school, the church, the sugar factory, the overseers quarters, the court and police stations – these are parts of the past to dislike because they were places for colonising people.

The christening is as bright as the sun was on that day. I see it as clearly as I see the ingredients of my cooking. The steam from the pots forms a mist. It rises in the air and I see more of the christening. It is very very hot but the men are wearing suits and ties. I pour the boiling water over the salt fish. I toss cloves and cinnamon sticks, orange peel and dark sugar into the hot, scarlet sorrel liquid.

I can see my father's trunk again – an ancient possession of his. This trunk came from somewhere far away. My father always tells me which country, but I always forget. He came from three, or more. He was born in one, one brought him here and several adopted him. I am a child again, struggling to drag it from under the bed. The handle is thin, black metal, very loose in my small hands. Every time I pull it towards me, from under my parents' bed, I think I am pulling a country towards me. I like to pull it out and open it, over and over. I always think I never know what I am going to find. But whenever I open it, there are always the same things there: a strange, shining black suit with a high-collared jacket and a white shirt with a stiff collar and large cuffs. I have never seen him dressed in this suit but he kept it in the best condition. It was not a suit for wearing. It never left the trunk except to be cleaned and aired. When I was no longer a child, someone told me it was his father's suit. My grandfather may have made it, since he was a tailor. There were papers in the trunk that I would secretly play with, because he said they were very important – yellowed, browning paper tied in pink string. He also kept there the letters he and my mother wrote each other when they were courting. Sometimes, my mother kept a dress for best there too, but not for long. All our birth certificates were kept in the trunk and mothballs too, to preserve everything.

We rarely had occasion for dressing up, only for births, marriages and deaths. Then our Sunday best came out of the trunk, out of the mothballs. Special occasions smelt of mothballs, of best soap, talcum, perfumes and new dresses. We always cleaned and washed ourselves – and everything else besides – for the new born, the newly wed and the dead.

The smell of ripe plantain is strongest in the pot of boiling cassava, yam, plantain and sweet potatoes. For the curry, I have to blend fresh pepper and jeera very lightly. The gravy has to be extremely thin. I must use only one fresh tomato and a leaf of thyme. Add water at the very last. I can see my mother dip a spoon into a karahi of boiling curry, trickle the gravy from a height so it cools in the air in its passage to the palm of her hand. I am in her kitchen again. She would never taste from the spoon, only from her palm. I trickle metagee into my palm but taste from hers. I am cooking for ghosts, spirits. The smell of my food is attracting them. For this very reason, there is no cooked food on the day of a funeral. The rituals of cooking, the opening of trunks smelling of mothballs, soap, perfume and talcum powder were part of the christening.

At the christening all the girls are in organza dresses. Mine is the palest colour of pink. I wear a small, white pillbox hat and white gloves. I am not just any child today, I am a godmother. My mother and father are there, and the Allens, and the baby, all the village. I can see the table, full of food. Today, I am cooking the same meal they prepared for the christening.

★ ★ ★ ★

My relatives arrive before my guests of honour. The scent of the food puts them in a good mood, makes them forget the cold weather, and stirs their memory.

The Allens lived in Cumberland all their lives until they went to live in Georgetown, in 1966. People were always leaving the country areas for Georgetown but I never thought they would leave.

"And they never came back to visit?"

"Oh yes!"

"But I never saw Yvette again."

"When they came to visit, you were always at school."

"No one told me when they visited."

"After the race riots, Joseph joined the new government, and stopped coming to Berbice. But he always wrote to your parents, he kept in touch."

"I never knew that. I used to ask after Yvette, and nobody ever told me that."

"There was an English priest who did the christening. Father Mason. He still in Berbice?"

"He was from the North of England. He was a paedophile. Everybody knew about it. I would not have him christen my child."

Secrets are the difficult parts of memory, especially secrets you are still not permitted to know, still not permitted to speak, secrets that were knowledge and power to protect the ones in control. You dare to speak them and they silence you with public shaming and ridicule. Secrets, knowledge and power were for closing ranks, keeping in the ones who never tell and keeping out the ones who do. Father Mason is dead now. We do not live in his parish. Our jobs do not depend on baptisings, christenings, masses, evensongs and funerals. His secret is not important any more. They can tell it now. But God is not dead. God might hear. Be careful. If you say it, say it once, and we will pretend we did not hear. There are places where there are echoes we cannot drown – places of the past, places of the mind, places of the heart.

When the doorbell rings I will open the front door and it will be as if memory is opening. The past and present will be joined.

The doorbell is ringing.

⋆ ⋆ ⋆ ⋆

Certainly their faces hardly bear a resemblance to the faces in my memory. They greet us with religious words. They are born-again Christians. Their mission is conversion. Before the meal, they say grace. Joseph behaves like a god. He expects women to wait on him, and Yvette and Cynthia do. He is a man of power. He was a policeman. Yvette and her mother hardly eat or speak, only when he prompts them.

Did I expect the ghosts would rise like Lazarus from the dead? Round and round the table goes the conversation. Guyana was now the second poorest country in the world after Haiti and malaria had returned; it was no longer the 'bread basket' of the Caribbean; no longer had the highest literacy rate in the region; our political culture was in ruins; we could not return home. Joseph nods like a president. They ask him questions about Guyana, the kind of anxious questions emigrants ask.

"How are things in Guyana?"

"Oh very good."

"Are the police still killing the opposition?"

"Oh no."

"Has the race politics stopped?"

"Oh yes."

"Are the roads improving?

"Oh yes."

"Has malaria really come back?"

"Oh no."

"Is there still a food shortage?"

"Oh no."

"You are a good public relations man for the country!"

"Oh yes indeed I am. After all I am the Chief of Police in Berbice."

Finally, only the fruit salad and black cake remained – the last fragments of the dream meal. On and on they talk about Guyana – the politics, the power struggles and hatreds without end. Joseph dictated the conversation. They could share no other memory with him.

Before they started on the black cake I had to perform the ritual. I don't know which I was – my mother or my young self. Perhaps both. Perhaps it was something to do with my father's trunk, but although I can see that Joseph did not like it, I went on speaking. I was telling Yvette I was sorry I never got to see her again, and I opened her hand and placed in it the pair of earrings I had bought for her. It was the right ritual. This is what you do for a godchild. You give gifts that last.

Her father spoke directly to her. "Yvette, you are very lucky indeed to have such a nice godmother. I hope you are grateful. You know, the young people are never grateful. You are very lucky to be born to have such a godmother. Those are good gold earrings, worth plenty. Let me see them."

He does not give her back her earrings. We clear the table. Joseph does not help. He throws his arm over the back of the chair and crosses his legs.

The time comes for them to leave and Joseph asks to speak to me privately. I take him to the kitchen.

"Maybe you live in England too long, and you don't remember. But it is the custom for the godparent to also give a present of money to the godchild father."

"My present is for Yvette, not for you."

I clear away the remains of my dream dinner. I wash the plates, cooker, and walls and surfaces of the kitchen. Yet, I am certain I detect a lingering scent of mothballs in the air.

REBIRTH

Nurse 1: "Open your eyes and look at me. I need to check your blood pressure again. Are you still dreaming?"

Nurse 2 : "The doctor said we must get her out of the anaesthetic. She opens her eyes but she can't speak. Speak to her again."

Nurse 1: "You've been semi-conscious since yesterday. You're due for a painkiller in fifteen minutes. Would you like it now? It will hurt for a bit."

No more drugs. I gave the frogs chloroform.

Nurse 2: "What did she say?"

Nurse 1: "Something about chloroform. Careful, don't touch her tubes."

I can hear Miss K.

Nurse 2 : "What did she say?"

Nurse 1: "She's delirious."

Say thanks to Father Mason for putting a blessing on you.

Nurse 2: "I can't understand a word, can you? It sounds like Pidgin English."

Miss K, the voodoo priestess put something, the good voodoo, wrapped in a handkerchief in a corner of the bed. It is supposed to make me get better. She says, Good herbs, chile, to make you get better. This is no voodoo.

Patient 1: "Can't you hear how distressed she is? Somebody wake her."

Miss K is saying, you need a good African burial to give

your jumbie peace. A Christian burial is no use to our jumbies. Miss K can say Hindu prayers too, do puja. Only she can bury me the Indian and African way, no Christian ways. Bring the hearse to put the corpse in ice. Let Sadhu come and tell me again that when I die the quicker I forget my body the better, that cremation is better than burial for *shukshma sharira*. Sadhu, what is *shukshma sharira*?

That is the four functions of your mind, Beti, and the winds of your body, and your five working organs and five knowledge organs.

Mother is saying, Sadhu is a heathen. Let him go and live in India if he wants to be an Indian. This is the West Indies, we are British. You will have an English funeral, so that you can go to heaven. Call Father Mason to preach a good sermon for you and bury you with holy water. You must die a Christian.

In my dreams, I see Mother moving from one room to another. Each room is different. Each is a different continent. Her spirit is wandering because Father Mason gave her communion wine and the body of Christ. She is not in Heaven because Sadhu and Miss K did not get to bury her and put Dutch pennies on her eyes. She should not have let Father Mason put communion wine on the lips of her corpse. I need Dutch pennies for the eyes of my corpse so I will not wander. Miss K will put Dutch pennies on my eyes. Sadhu will put red tikka on my third eye. Send for Miss K.

She is dead.

When? Where?

Ten years ago, alone in her cottage in South America. Pass four culverts. Go to her. They did not give her a Christian burial. They were afraid to bury her. The voodoo spirits came and took her away.

Miss K, I have come for you to bury me. Look, nothing has changed. Twenty years I was away, come back dead and nothing changed. Miss K, I come. You look so young.

Oh my darling, you come to see me?

Yes, don't tell Mother. Don't tell Father Mason. They will want to bury me.

Don't worry about Mother. Mother is not here. She is dead. She died before you.

The anaesthetist said he is from Barbados so I tell him to go and call Miss K.

All right darling, all right darling, I will go and get her, you just count to five and you will go to sleep and have real sweet dreams.

No counting even, next thing I know, I am in the elevator, going back to the ward and smelling of chloroform and almost dead. We used chloroform to put frogs to sleep in the school laboratory before we cut them and they cut me.

Nurse 1: "Who is Miss K? She keeps calling for Miss K."

She is Miss Koko, a Cromati woman. Father Mason tried to jail her.

Nurse 3 : "Wake up. I have to take your blood pressure."

This is a nurse. Concentrate. Wake yourself up. Live. This is a nurse. Open your eyes and look. Don't be afraid to open your eyes. No Dutch pennies for my eyes. I must not die without Dutch pennies for my eyes. This girl has no Dutch pennies for my eyes. But her eyes are blue like the Dutchman's eyes. She is his daughter. Tell her to go and ask him for Dutch pennies for my eyes. Her eyes are too blue. Look out, Dutchman haunt Guyana. Dutchman left all his gold Dutch pennies buried in jars all over Guyana. If you find the pennies, never spend it. You must only use it to bury the dead or the blue-eye Dutchman will kill you.

Nurse 3 : "You must keep your arm still. I am trying to take your blood pressure."

Your husband has gone home, they said. Husbands are supposed to stay with their dead. You do not leave the dead on their own. You are supposed to sit up with the dead one night and one day. When Grandmother died, the whole family came from all over the world and formed a circle round her bed for one night and one day. They never left her side.

"Why has he gone home?"

Nurse 1: "She is speaking, at last. Call matron! Call the doctor!"

Nurse 3 : "Sorry to wake you up again."

They do not leave the dead alone to die in peace. They harass the dead.

"My back hurts."

Nurse 1: "Her back hurts. She wants something for pain."

No more drugs. I reek of chloroform. Why are you giving me chloroform?

"Sick, sick."

Nurse 1: "Get her a bowl."

"Pain."

Nurse 2: "I'm sorry but you can only have an injection for the pain every four hours. You can have a pill every two hours."

"Hot."

Patient 1: "Someone get her a fan! Tell the nurse to get her a fan. Sweat is pouring from her."

No fan. Don't give me a fan. Uncle Darcus hung himself near his fan. He always sat in front of the fan. When he hung himself he kept the fan on. I don't want the fan. Take the fan away.

Nurse 1: "She's coming out of the anaesthetic."

Nurse 2: "Hello dear, do you speak English?"

You must tell them you speak English. Make them know you understand them.

"Yes."

Nurse 1: "She's fully conscious now."

Nurse 3: "You're in intensive care. This afternoon the doctor will be down to see you."

★ ★ ★ ★

Nurse 2: "Are you awake? The doctor has something to tell you."

Doctor: "I am sorry, but we must operate again this afternoon. We must do a special test immediately."

Miss K says once they cut you, you is no good no more. After all these white people never think about the soul. They only treat your body, cutting it up, cutting it up and they think it will live. Stupidy people. They don't know to get better. You must dance till the spirit catch you and throw you down. How you can dance if they cut you up?

"No, not so soon, too soon."

Doctor: "I assure you, there is no danger."

★ ★ ★ ★

Doctor: "Stand aside nurse!"

Doctor: "Breathe in deeply and hold your breath!"

Nurse 3 : "Are you in pain? "

"Yes."

Blue-eye jumbie white girl, Dutchman daughter, go and bring the pennies for my eyes now.

Nurse 3: "Is it bad? Think of something nice."

Too many voices.

Doctor: "Take a deep breath. Nurse, stand aside."

Nurse 3 :"I'll come back. Bear up now."

The machine rumbles and clicks and too much pain.

Doctor: "Thank you. Breathe normally."

The blue-eyed nurse comes back. She cradles my head.

Nurse 3: "Think of something nice, the nicest thing that you've done. Go on, think about the thing that makes you happiest. What about swimming in the Caribbean Sea? Imagine it. I know someone from the Caribbean, he's a nurse here. He's lovely. When were you last in the Caribbean? Are you still in pain?"

Doctor: "Stand aside Nurse! Another deep breath and hold!"

Nurse 3 : "It's all right."

Her voice ebbs and flows like water.

Nurse 3 : "Don't close your eyes. Look at me. Take deep, gentle breaths. I'm here. Try to relax. Is the pain bad?"

The pain is too bad. I am dying. I can hear her voice, and Miss K's voice too.

Nurse 3 : "Doctor, she is in pain. It's the drain. You shut it off. Can I turn it on again?"

Doctor : "We'll hurry. We need to take several pictures. We have to find the leak. We'll be as quick as we can. Deep breath! Hold! Breathe! Deep breath! Hold! Breathe deeply! Deep breath! Hold! Breathe! Deep breath! Hold! Breathe! Two more, then it'll be over!"

I am in the jumbie grave now, drowning in it like Miss K says happens when you die and like the time Uncle Darcus threw me into the trench to make me swim. When my body hit the water, I thought I would bounce off it and be safe but it parted for me like cloth, then next thing I know I am weightless, the water is soaking through me and I can see underwater the bodies of the other children who are swimming. Where are my brothers? My mother has sent them to tea at Father Mason while I am drowning and dying. Underwater it is not brown but grey. My eyes will die first because the water is hurting them. If I shut my eyes I won't see myself dying. When I die again I will shut my eyes so I can't see myself doing it. I get to the bottom of the water and my feet and hands touch the mud. It is soft soft mud, like mud at the bottom of the graves where the jumbies live, the kind of mud I would have had to live in if I died and let the jumbies put me in the grave. Fight the water and live. Move, move, move, push, push the water, push back the pain in the chest, in the head, until they come to save you, human hands like the white girl hands saving you now. Don't cry, not now, not then. They were all laughing because they knew I nearly died. My eyes are open and I am living. Her face is there, not the water, not the ceiling.

Again she says, look at me, keep your eyes open. I look and see her eyes blue blue blue blue blue blue blue like the midday sky at home and blue like Father Mason's eyes. Home is in her blue eyes. She tells me the sun is hot. I am at home. She tells me I am in the Caribbean. She tells me I am swimming in the sea; it is warm and comforting and relaxing in the water; she tells me I am at home. All my friends and family and the people I love are there. She wants me to live. She is afraid to see me die. She does not know how to let me die. How blue the sky in her eyes, how cool the breeze at home where I belong, how sad not to be at home. Her fingers brush my cheek. I am not fainting. I am going to sleep, like a baby. Like a mother, she is rocking and coaxing me to sleep. There is no pain. I am not dying. I lose the memory to fight. I let her hold my hand. I go to sleep. I take her hand with me to sleep, feeling safe to sleep.

★ ★ ★ ★

I can hear the distant noises of other rooms and wards and offices in the hospital. I will leave this quiet room and return to my real life and remember everything. Turn. See? My head moves, it is alive. There is a nurse at a desk. Don't die, call the nurse.

"Nurse!"

Call again. "Nurse!"

She is coming.

"Yes?"

"I don't feel very well."

She comes closer. "What is it, my love?"

"I feel really bad."

"Well it's not surprising, your insides have been handled twice now in two major operations in two days. We've been trying desperately to get you to come round."

"What was this operation?"

"To repair your urethra. It was a reimplantation of the right urethra, near your bladder; it was leaking. They had to take you straight from the x-ray because you fainted while they were taking the pictures. You have had a lot of anaesthetic you know. You have been very delirious, talking and arguing with everybody, in a world of your own. You have been worrying us. You'll be all right now."

The clock says three o' clock. I remember I had a mother who died. She died now, at three o' clock in the morning and the priest she believed in never once came to see her or give her the last rites. I am not dead yet. No mother, not time for you to come for me. That is what the people Father Mason called heathens used to say, that when it is time for me to die, my mother will call me. I will see her and she will come for me. Not God, not Jesus, your mother. I musn't sleep or else I will die and she and Father Mason will come for me. Stay awake, doze a little, wake again, doze again. Don't go to sleep and dream or you will die.

The feel of cold flannel on face. A blessing.

"Joanna?"

"Who is Joanna, my darling baby girl?"

Another dream. Open my eyes. This is Miss K, leaning over me and smiling. Miss K why you take so long to come? They said you were dead.

"Miss K, what you doing here? "

"Lord child, you could really talk in your sleep. All the time you talking. I can't understand you half the time and they send me because they say I will understand you. They say you talking West Indies. They say you talking voodoo. Careful, chile, or else they will lock you up. This is a Christian country. I will leave the bowl of water here and the flannel and come and wipe your face for you later. Where you from? I from Grenada."

"I can't remember. Find out for me."

"Look, right here your notes say you are a Christian and we should send for the priest. You dreaming. You calling in your sleep. Whole night you calling. Poor baby girl. Go back to sleep now. Is the anaesthetic. You had it plenty times. It will wear off and you will remember everything. Rest."

Lights out. Blanket of sleep. Trolleys going by. Doctors. Silence. More trolleys. Silence. Noise. Marching. Noise of marching feet. Nurses coming and going. Trolleys and porters and corpses. Echoes. I look just like my mother as I die. She was lying in the most well-made bed. The sheets and blanket looked as if they had been ironed round her.

* * * *

"Hello. Wake up. How're you feeling? I am sorry. We have to operate on you a third time. I'm the anaesthetist. Just another anaesthetic. Does anaesthetic affect you?"

Nurse 1: "Your husband is here."

When she was dying, Mother used to call for me, and they used to tell her: *your daughter is coming.* I can remember I had a mother but I don't remember her face because she had no Dutch pennies for her eyes.

"What's this they're telling me about you having to go back to the theatre? "

"My mind is getting straight."

"This has nothing to do with your mind. It's about your body. Where is the doctor?"

Nurse 2: "Yes sir, of course, I'll get the doctor."

Nurse 1: "We're going to give you your premed now."

Nurse 2 : "Would you like Nurse Carew to do it, Joanna Carew?"

"I don't want more anaesthetic, again, so soon."

Nurse Carew: "You're going to feel very drowsy now. Don't worry. I'm here. You can talk to me. Listen to me. You're not going to die. And I'll be here when you get back from the theatre, and if I'm not on duty, I'll come and see you. I promise."

The anaesthetist: " I'm just going to give you an injection now. It'll put you to sleep. Count to five."

Pull me out of the dark hole where I am curled up like a foetus. No one hears me calling. The nurse who looks like Miss K is wearing her white uniform. She is walking in the hospital corridor. She is carrying a bowl of water for my face. I am calling her but my voice is choked in my throat, like when Uncle Darcus threw me into the trench and I nearly drowned. But I could hear them laughing kyah kyah kyah. I was in the water but I could still hear them. I want to get out. I smell of chloroform. Your mother is in a coma, come at once. I must get out. Push. Swim. Push. Once more. Push. The head is almost there. I can't push any more. I'm dead. One more time. Your baby is ready. I want you to do the last stage breathing. Pant pant pant. Push hard when I say, not before. I see the head. You are at home. The sky is blue in her eyes. Push. After you die you will be alive. Give her oxygen. Hold her tubes. Breathe. Pant. Push. Push. Come on. Yes yes yes yes yes. There we are, there.

* * * *

"It's me, Joanna. Open your eyes and look at me."

Her eyes are the colour of the sky at home; her hand is soft, too soft to cut the navel string. Miss K know how to cut the navel string.

"Pull me out."

"Take my hand. I'm here. Let me wipe your face. You poor thing. You are having a difficult time. This was the last operation. Your urethra has been opened."

My mother's womb opened again. I was born again.

" Keep still, or else you'll disconnect the tubes. You'll fall off the bed."

Hold her Miss K, she falling. Jumbie got her. Don't let me catch you going to the voodoo dances. People go into trances and fall down and you got to hold them down. Miss K is the obeah woman, she does hold them down and put cloth between they teeth to stop the fits. They always get better afterwards.

"There, there. I'm holding your hand. Open your eyes. That's it. Keep them open. Look at me and try and remember what is happening to you. Don't close your eyes. Open them. You must wake up."

"They finished the x-ray?"

"This isn't the x-ray. That was yesterday. You must try to wake up now. You've been delirious, hallucinating. Look I brought you a card, and a present. Do you like anemones?"

"Flowers."

"Yes, they're English, like me. I'm from Henley, you know, where they have the regatta. I was born there, lived there all my life before coming to London two years ago."

"I died again and was born too."

"Hush. Try and talk sense."

"My husband was born here. I had his baby. I remember having a baby."

"He came but you were sleeping. He went away but he'll be back."

When Mother was dying, her sister-in-law kept wanting to see her although they hated each other. Miss K says your enemies have to come and pay their respects to you when you are dying so you will not blow a bad breeze on them.

"It's the anaesthetic and painkillers. You've had a lot of both. You're drugged. It'll wear off in a day or two. I'll wash your face. Here. Is that good? "

"Yes. Again. My neck too."

"Turn over, I'll do your back."

I was an infant. We are all bathing together, girls and women and babies. Lily is holding me. She is stooping. I am naked, on her knee. She is drenched in her dress and she is pouring calabashfuls of water over me. This is the bath-house over the river. It's a small weather-beaten hut on a platform made of large wooden planks. All the women come here to bathe together with the children. When they want to bathe naked they go into the hut and I can see them soaping themselves there. White soapsuds trail along their bodies. They pour water over each other. I am taken there to be soaped then brought out again to be rinsed clean. There are several buckets of water and everyone dips into them. Lily lifts me high into the air and I can see the huge trees of the forest around us as the women take turns to fill the buckets. The ritual of washing goes on for a very long time. It is the earliest memory I have of myself now, now that I am born again.

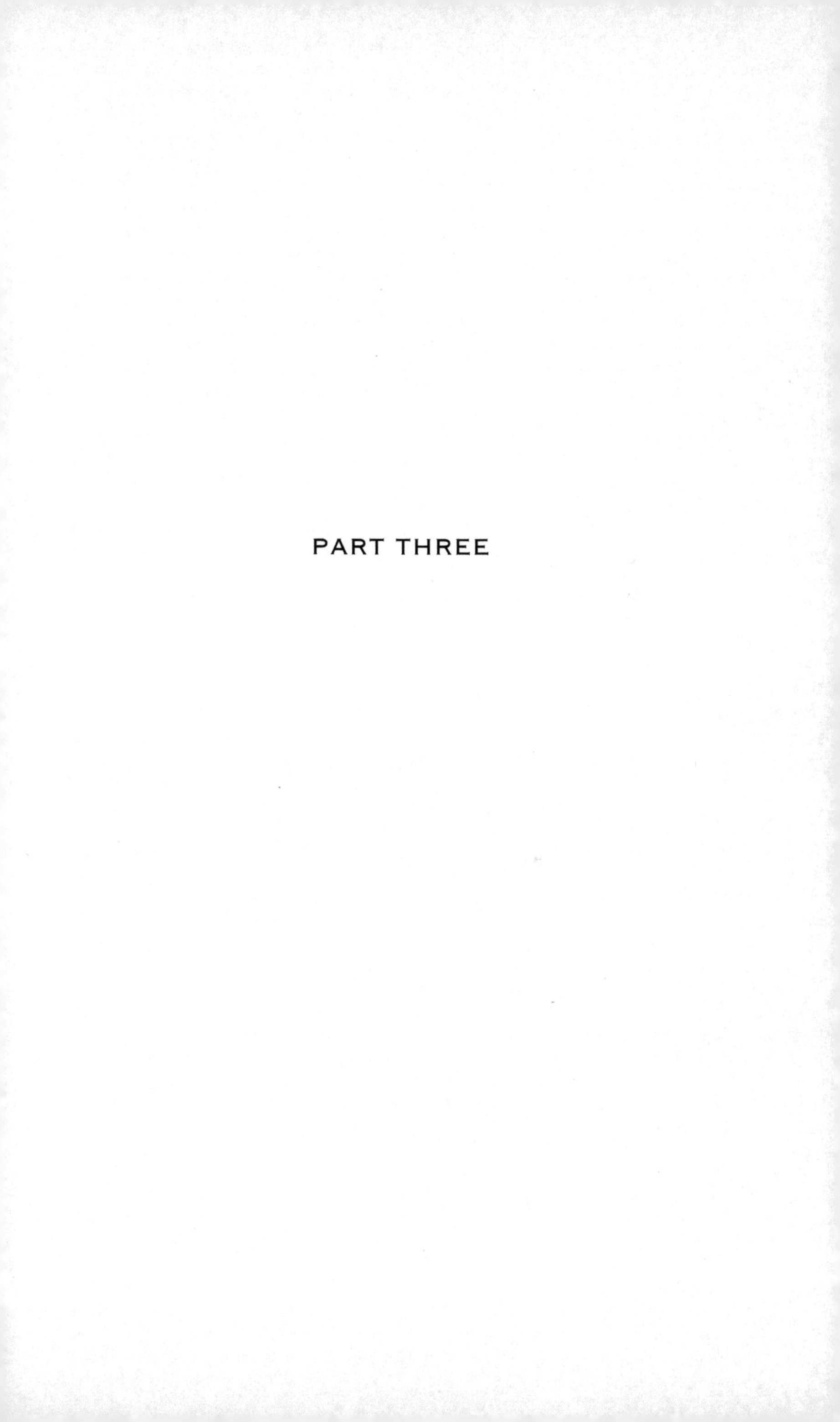

PART THREE

LONDON AND NEW YORK

Soho, London

Instead of listening to my order, the waiters at The Canton in London's Soho listened to my accent and strained to place it. I used to have to repeat the order twice, even thrice. I used to catch them looking at me with intense curiosity. However, in ten years they have not asked if I am from China, Hong Kong, Malaysia, Singapore, or the Philippines. Now they accept I am a woman who likes to come here to eat. Now, the headwaiter greets me like an old friend, serves me himself and gives me his warmest smile.

I go to Soho, too, to meet different friends, to catch up on our different interests. We meet at Cranks Restaurant in Great Newport Street because there is no limit on the time they let us spend there, nor do they monitor how much we spend drinking just tea and coffee.

The Canton reminds me of my grandmother's cooking in old British Guiana. She was Chinese. Her first husband was a man from Kashmir who died young; then a man from Delhi became her devoted husband. He spoke Hindi, so did she. So did we. She wore saris he bought her as tokens of his love. Once a week, they went to the cinema to watch romantic Indian films and learn the latest love songs by Latamangeshkar. He taught her to cook Indian dishes –

where to buy the spices and how and when to use them – to grow all the vegetables herself, to raise her own ducks and chickens. She made delicious duck curry. I used to chase the ducks around the garden and catch them so she could thank Allah and bless the duck while she slit its throat, drained the blood, and placed it in a tub of scalding water for the children to strip the feathers.

So while I sit at my table at The Canton, I am a secure child again in British Guiana. I am with my brothers and sister. We are chasing ducks around our backyard. I hear my grandmother trying to sing like Latamangeshkar in a Guyanese accent. I am enjoying the memory of my Delhi-born stepgrandfather, who was an affectionate man who, when he visited, always remembered to bring a present for each of his stepchildren and stepgrandchildren. When I eat roast duck and Chinese greens at The Canton in London, I taste East Indian duck in their Chinese duck, I taste Guyanese calaloo in Chinese greens. In my memory, I am in a Guyanese garden.

Southall, London

I have a long journey to The Canton so I don't go as often as I would like. It takes thirty to forty-five minutes on London's Piccadilly Line. However, Omi's restaurant is local. It takes me ten minutes from my home in West London to drive there. I have eaten there for as long as I have at The Canton. There is no better Punjabi food in Southall, especially the curried fish, pilau rice and bhindi. Guyanese curries were part of the Creole diet I grew up with – though they bear little resemblance to Punjabi cooking.

Kuldip first took me there in the early eighties. He introduced me to the owners – several brothers and their father whose BMWs were always parked in the forecourt.

When Kuldip wanted to treat comrades or journalists from the BBC or the national newspapers, he took them to Omi's. It took a couple of months for the penny to drop – they used to smile at me because they thought I was his girlfriend. When I began to turn up alone, at first I got the same curious, overprotective looks the waiters at The Canton used to give me.

At lunchtime, it used to be all English – packed with teachers and local government staff. Those were the days of Ken Livingstone's Greater London Council when Southall attracted the white Left. It also used to attract the Black and Asian Left because it was once a front line town like Brixton, when it fought racists off its streets.

At teatime, the students from the tertiary college and secondary schools fill the restaurant. They do all the things they can't do at home or in the streets where their elders can see them. They chat up boyfriends and girlfriends. They smoke, they drink beer. They listen to *hip-hop*, *gangster rap*, *ragga*, and *jungle* on their ghetto blasters. They live in Southall and environs – Punjabis mainly, but also Muslims, Somalis, English, Irish, African, Caribbean, Vietnamese, Chinese. In those days, I used to teach at the tertiary college.

In the weekdays and on weekends, large extended Punjabi families come for early dinner.

In between lunch, tea, and dinner, it is quieter. I take my friends then, and we take as long as we like drinking cups of massala tea and mop the gravy and chutney on our plates with the last piece of chapati or tandoori naan.

In old British Guiana, my father used to travel a long way to town for Chinese cooking – although he ran his own eating-place. It was divided in two, the cake shop on the left and grocery on the right. On market days the women monopolised the cake shop when they came to cool their thirst on their way home. Then, the men had to use the grocery. On Saturday mornings, the women came to the grocery – then, the men had to use the cake shop. In the canecutting season, the whole place was a refuge for canecutters. In the mornings, it was full of workmen wanting cigarettes and loaves of bread and cheese to take to the factory and fields. In father's place, it was the times when the barriers came down that he liked, the times you would find men and women, children and adults, not in an exclusive space, but talking to each other.

Brixton, London

Mother's menu included fufu, metagee, peas and rice, plantains, yams, cassavas, eddoes, tanya, breadfruit, pepperpot made with fermented casareep, salt fish, salt beef, konki. Her menu weaned me off breast milk. She also used it to teach me to cook for myself. Friends come to my table expecting Chinese. I have to explain that I prefer to eat Chinese at The Canton and Indian at Omi's because cooking them does not come to me as naturally as African Guyanese cooking.

I lived in London for over twenty-five years before I found a restaurant with a menu as evocative of my mother's tastes and lifestyle as The Canton's was of my grandmother and Omi's of my father. It took so long because I never looked for one. London was famous for its Indian and Chinese restaurants, not Caribbean ones. So I always cooked my mother's favourite dishes at home, for my family, friends and myself.

Shopping for the ingredients was as integral to their power to evoke the memory of my mother as was cooking them – although she grew everything in her garden. Her gardening involved an intricate communal system: seeds, roots, shoots and their harvest, all exchanged between neighbours. When I travel to Finsbury Park, Shepherd's

Bush or Brixton to find the ingredients for my mother's menu, I relive the journeys she and her friends would make *down the road* in search of a better crop of cassava or tanya root to bring back to their gardens, replant and harvest for their cooking.

The first time I went to Cafe Jam in Brixton, the friend who took me there had no idea the chef and the menu were Guyanese. We were hungry and it was the nearest restaurant so we dropped in and made a snap decision to have lunch there. The waitress told us if we were willing to wait, she had to go *down the road* to Brixton market to bring in some of the ingredients. When our meal arrived, it was cooked in the Guyanese style, down to the black cake dessert. Now I eat at Cafe Jam regularly and I am really happy when I have to wait a long time for the ingredients to be brought in from *down the road*.

Chinatown, New York

For the first time in New York, I was trying to find my way to Chinatown to find the red bean cakes my mother made. I asked a young woman the way. As she gave me directions I heard the unmistakable accent of someone from the Dominican Republic. As soon as she had given me directions she then said, "You have an English and a Caribbean accent." She wished me a good day and went on her way, waving to me as she disappeared into the crowd. It reminded me how Caribbean people have developed the skills of cultural translation. We tune our ears to accents, learning to recognise and use them to map our everyday transactions. Without that skill and other ones, we would have no maps to negotiate with. So, on my way to Chinatown I was reminded by a woman from the Caribbean that I was from the Caribbean, though I was looking for the home that my mother's red bean cake symbolised in Chinatown in New York, which I was visiting for the first time.

Eventually, I got to Chinatown. As I walked around, it struck me how different New York's Chinatown is from London's. For one, there was the aggressive competition for space between the tall buildings, automobiles, and people who were dwarfed like ants by everything. I missed London's narrow streets. Here were people running for their lives as they crossed the road, drivers oblivious to their safety. It made me think of wild west movies, of wagons and horses stampeding through town and terrorising people. In the mannerisms of some of the people of Chinatown I saw the inflections of the wild west too – the macho John Wayne swagger in the way the owners of the jewellery shops guarded their trays of gold in open view of the pavement – daring anyone to a high noon shootout. I saw the Marlon Brando curl of the lips when they spoke.

But I did not give up on my mother's red bean cake. I ventured to ask for them in a cake shop. I was shown red bean cakes I had never seen before, and the proprietor and I talked about the differences between the cakes I buy in London's Soho and the cakes on display in his shop. I explained to him that in London I always got my mother's red bean cakes from a shop in Soho. We were translating to each other the specificities of our different locations by talking about Chinese cakes. Cakes had become a metaphor of home to both of us. It gave me the confidence to explore a bit more, to get beyond the John Wayne and Marlon Brando macho barrier guarding the border to New York. And I came home with a bag of food much better for my diet than red bean cakes: a bag full of beautifully fresh pak choi, string beans, and spring onions, amazed at how much cheaper they are here and how much you get for a dollar. I paid three dollars for a bag of vegetables that would have set me back about eight pounds in London, that is, eleven dollars. New York wasn't so bad.

Later that night, I found red bean cakes, exactly like my mother's, in a Guyanese restaurant in Brooklyn. In London I get red bean cakes in Chinatown but not in Guyanese restaurants. In New York I do not find them in Chinatown but in a Guyanese restaurant in Brooklyn.

THE BERBICE MARRIAGE MATCH

"Arrange a marriage match," Alexander Choy told his mother.

Schoolteacher Elizabeth Waldron wrote the letter on their behalf.

His mother came late one afternoon and stayed from beginning to end to witness the writing. Her eyes were black as the ink, and she observed closely each stroke and loop of the moving pen until the page was full of words.

It was four o' clock in the afternoon. They were sitting in the Waldron family kitchen. Elizabeth had come in from teaching all day to find Clarice Choy waiting patiently for her on the front landing. Before writing the letter, she had put some plantains and other ground provisions to boil. Now, with the kitchen moist with steam from the cooking pot, she reflected, as she wrote, that Alexander could have written the letter himself. After all, she taught him to read and write. His handwriting was just like hers, full of italic flourishes. But it was the Chinese custom for the mother to negotiate.

"Mrs. Choy, what do you want me to say about Alexander?"

"Nothing 'bout Alexander. Say to come he' three week time, she an' daughte'. Say it nice, write nice letter."

So she wrote:

Mrs. Clarice Tsue Choy,
Plantation Rose Hall Village,
Canje District,
Berbice County.
5th of March 1944

Mrs. Enid Li,
4 Light Street,
Albertown,
Georgetown,
Demerara County.

Dear Mrs. Li,

I trust that my letter will find you enjoying the best of health and God's Blessings.

May I extend my gracious thanks to you for your letter of 15th of February 1944 instant and enclosure of the photograph of your eldest respected daughter Ruth Felicity Li with whom you ask to arrange a marriage match with my eldest son, Alexander Theophilus Choy.

I have the greatest pleasure in informing you that I will be pleased to receive a visit from yourself and your daughter at a time befitting your convenience to be arranged at the above address.

Please inform me in advance the date of your impending visit in order that our family can make the proper arrangements to receive you.

Thanking You In Anticipation,
I Remain,
Your Humble Servant,
Mrs. Clarice Tsue Choy

Instead of cash payment for the letter, Elizabeth accepted the promise of a Christmas cake to be baked and delivered on the 24th of December. The Choy family was famous for their baking. Ovens were a luxury. The overseers bought special all-in-one ones from England. Local people used wood-fired ovens or stoves that used up as much as a gallon of kerosene to do one round of baking in four hours – expensive and time consuming. Alexander had built a large wood-fired clay oven where he was to be seen every Friday shovelling trays of Creole and Chinese cakes into its blasting hot interior: cassava pone, pine tarts, patties, rock buns, salara, cheese rolls, tennis rolls, and blackeye cake. It was customary for a large audience to gather in their front yard each Friday under the shading guinep tree to gossip, play cards and dominoes, and consume the cakes fresh, hot and just out of the oven, washing them all down with his mother's home-made iced mauby and sorrel drinks. At Christmas, the oven took ten 2lb fruit cakes at one go.

★ ★ ★ ★

The letter was dispatched to Georgetown without Clarice's other children – Winston or Shirley – knowing about the match. However, they spied the photograph of Alexander's intended, where he had placed it, near his bed, next to photos of film stars Claudette Colbert and Jane Wyman. They asked about the girl in the photograph.

★ ★ ★ ★

In Georgetown, Mrs. Li also kept the letter secret from her three girls at home, Lilith, Evelyn, and Rebecca. Fortunately, the postman delivered it to her rented room in Light Street after they left for school or else she would have had to explain why she was not opening it for them to read to her. She tucked it into her bosom and headed towards Brickdam for the Chinese Association where she worked. She stopped in at Brickdam Cathedral to ask Father Del Pino to read the letter. He not only read it, he told her to be sure to arrange a Catholic wedding for Ruth.

Rain fell early that morning but the sun was out now and drying everything. Yesterday's heat and dust were gone. The oleander and bougainvillaea looked beautiful, with their leaves, branches and flowers beaded with sunlight and rainwater. People were enjoying the coolness in the air.

At work, she sang over the ironing and wondered why. After all, it was not easy to raise four girls without a son or husband to help you face the world. There were more dowries to be scrimped and scraped, more matchmaking to be done for the other three. A good marriage for Ruth was important. She needed it more than any of the girls because she was the only one to be fostered out of their home.

In the evening, Mrs. Li walked back to Albertown, tired, but with the letter still near her heart.

A week passed with her setting off each morning with the letter in her bosom, intending to visit Ruth at the home of her foster family and tell her about the marriage match. But each afternoon, she failed to do it. Finally, Ruth came home on her weekly visit and then Enid broke the news and revealed the letter. It was a shock. They had no idea their mother had asked the Chinese Association to select a family in Berbice or that she asked Father Del Pino to write them.

One by one, the girls rebelled. First Lilith: "Mother, this is the twentieth century. We are not living in the dark ages any more. People do not have arranged marriages any more. You only marry the person you love and choose."

Evelyn joined in: "Mother, we are Guianese now. We are Christian. I am not having a marriage match!"

Then Rebecca: "Mother, please do not pick my husband. I will pick him myself."

Mrs. Li went on the warpath: limited rations of meat with meals, more callaloo than usual in the egg soup, the furniture to be polished twice if it did not shine enough, dusting three times a week instead of two; no visits to the cinema that month; and lecture after lecture about the meaning of being Chinese. The Chinese were the most industrious people in the world; the Chinese invented everything from paper to counting, from gunpowder to silk; the world would be nowhere without the Chinese; the Chinese were the oldest civilisation in the world; Confucius, the Chinese philosopher, invented the civil service and civic society.

The girls had never heard talk like this. Here, the Chinese numbered only a few thousand. After all, their mother's mother came from China but left her orphaned, to be raised by Catholic nuns, without any Chinese customs; she had raised them as Catholics. What did she know about Chinese customs? Since when was it so important to be Chinese, or possible to be Chinese here in British Guiana? Enid had never told her daughters that she listened regularly to the public lectures on Chinese culture held at the Chinese Association. The Chinese community in Georgetown, being so tiny, knew her business. By way of helping her to bring up her four daughters, they gave her a generous salary for her services as cook and laundress, and the wives of the professional men liked to leave her anonymous parcels of food, books and clothing.

Three weeks after the letter arrived, the girls found themselves on the train to Berbice with their mother. It was the first time they had visited another part of the country. They took the 6 a.m. train, with the intention of returning on the 6 p.m.. They made a pretty picture – this petite Chinese woman and her four beautiful young daughters dressed in their Sunday best and smart hats, as they boarded the train in Carmichael and Lamaha Streets.

The train sped across the flat land. Village after village

appeared and disappeared – Plaisance, Buxton, Beterverwagting. You could see straight into people's backyards as the train passed through. There were coconut plantations, cattle farms, rice fields and American army jeeps on the public road. Wherever the train stopped, hucksters crowded round and tried to sell their trays of roti and curry, fried plantain and cassava, fried fish and bread with pepper sauce, phulourie, sugar apples, sapodillas, sugarcakes, konki and even black pudding and souse. By the time they reached Mahaicony, it was almost eight o'clock and the train was full of passengers. Everyone was talking at the same time. On and on the train sped through Abary, into the West Coast. The girls forgot their reason for going to Berbice – Enid too. She was enjoying herself eating all the different foods they bought. She ate roti with souse and sipped coconut water through a straw to cool the sting of the ball-of-fire pepper on her tongue.

British Guiana was such a big country; you had only to travel across the endless horizon and acres of sky to forget your problems and think they were really smaller than you thought. It occurred to Lilith that her mother was unsure the arranged marriage was the right thing and they stood a chance of making her change her mind. She told her sisters so and they agreed. They began to feel so optimistic they stuck their heads through the window to let the breeze play with their hair but their mother ordered them to stop after they leaned right out to try and pluck bananas off the trees. At Rosignol, they crossed the river in a steamer and got so excited, they made their mother lose her temper and order them to sit still and be quiet.

In New Amsterdam, Elizabeth Waldron met them at the stelling and explained that she had written the letter and acted as a go-between for Mrs. Choy since her English was not good. Mrs. Li began to feel nervous. That Mrs. Choy spoke poor English must be a sign of how Chinese she was.

Maybe she would think they were too Creole. Maybe the Choys did not come to British Guiana as labourers and would look down on her. Maybe Mrs. Choy would change her mind once she saw the whole family together, all female, with no man to look after them, their father having died when they were still small.

On the bus, Ruth began to cry, and this set off her sisters. As far as they were concerned, their mother was about to foster her a second time. When the bus stopped in Rose Hall, a miserable family emerged. Enid had to take only one look at Mrs. Choy to see she was in the presence of what must surely be a genuine Chinese. She was dressed in black silk pajamas and silk sandals, and her hair was swept back in a bun, not cut short and permed in the English style like hers.

Enid felt a little better to see that there was also no husband and father in the Choy family, but there were two sons, Winston as well as Alexander. Enid had longed for a son too but got four girls. The Choys were lined up along the stairs. Their mother instructed them to bow to their visitors. Enid bowed back, but not the girls. They just wept and clung to Ruth, making a complete fool of her. Clarice Choy looked so annoyed, Enid felt more and more ashamed, and struggled harder to keep her dignity.

They sat down to a Chinese meal. Immediately, Ruth knocked over the Chinese vase full of hibiscus flowers. It shattered on the immaculately polished floor. Clarice said nothing as she retrieved the broken pieces. Shirley arranged the flowers in another vase. After that, Alexander and his teacher tried to maintain some conversation. He made attempts to encourage the visitors to eat, but the broken vase hung like a ghost over the meal, depressing them. Except Alexander.

The studio photograph of Ruth was wooden and formal and made her look like a doll, but in the flesh she and her sisters were the most beautiful girls he had ever seen. He had fallen in love with Ruth the instant he saw her photograph. In the flesh, she was even more ravishing and his heart was bursting, his blood racing. Even though she was weeping, she did it in a sad, not a pathetic way. It showed how much she loved her family. It meant she would love him and their children too. Her face was strong as well as soft – just what he wanted in a wife. For all their show of fear and timidness, she and her sisters were only trying to make their mother do what they wanted. He had no doubt he wanted to marry her.

When it was time to clear the table, the Choys showed the Li family to the veranda. Clarice and Shirley served them coconut water, and soft and delicate pink and white sugarcakes.

There was a good view of the village, with the dark green canefields and cocoa brown canal running parallel on the wide horizon. The breeze blew in from the canefields and it was warm and scented with the perfume of cane and freshwater. There was more space here than in the crowded streets of Georgetown. There was a good-sized kitchen garden around each cottage and wide parapets along the paths where the men were playing cricket. It was Sunday. People were resting at home in their hammocks or forking and planting their gardens. There was the intoxicating smell of East Indian and Creole cooking in the air. They could hear a baby crying and the voices of children – perhaps boys climbing trees or plunging and swimming in the canals or the girls playing gutty or skipping.

While they took in all this, they could also hear the sounds of the Choys clearing the table, washing up. When their voices rose they could put together the occasional sentence well enough to hear that Winston and Shirley did not like them because they were not "real" Chinese, they were Creole. They had not shown the proper respect of bowing, of taking care to appear glad to meet them, and then they had broken their best piece of Chinese China and not offered to replace it. Enid Li burned with shame. She wanted to replace the vase but knew she might not find or afford a suitable one. She felt worse when her daughters asked her to explain what it was to be a "real" Chinese. She pretended not to hear their questions.

But Enid knew her girls, knew that now that they knew that the Choys were prejudiced, they would be even more determined and fight against Ruth marrying into this family. So, she decided that before Clarice Choy returned to cancel the match, she would do it first. She was thinking about how she would put it when Alexander's voice carried clearly on the breeze, declaring that Ruth was the only girl he was going to marry and, if necessary, he would abandon his own family and follow her to Georgetown.

Alexander was the favoured son. What he wanted counted. They all heard Clarice tell him to ignore his brother and sister; the match would go ahead. But Enid was proud. Before the Choys could return to the veranda, she told her daughters she was calling off the match.

Ruth was prouder than her mother. She was not going to let her family come all this way to be insulted. Canje was not a bad place. It was big and spacious. It was a good place to raise a family. It was somewhere her sisters and mother could visit to get away from Georgetown. It was time their luck turned. Who knows, perhaps Alexander would do so well, they would live in their own house and she would be able to look after her mother in her old age. He was very good looking. He seemed soft hearted and kind. His bakery was also doing very well. He was a breadwinner. He was his mother's favourite. He would defend her against Shirley and Winston. He could be the best husband she would get.

It was a shock for Enid when Ruth declared she was willing to accept Alexander, so when the Choys returned to the veranda the two matriarchs bowed very deeply to each other and their offspring were compelled to follow suite.

Elizabeth helped complete the formality of agreeing the dowry, the financial contribution each side would make to the wedding expenses and a consultation with a Chinese fortune-teller to set the best date for the wedding.

Alexander and Elizabeth accompanied the Li family back to the stelling. They went as far as crossing the river with them so that Alexander could take Ruth's hand and help her on to the 6 o' clock train.

ABOUT THE AUTHOR

Jan Lowe Shinebourne (nee Lowe) was born in Guyana on Rose Hall Sugar Estate. She attended school on the estate, and then Berbice High School. She comes from the same area of Guyana as her near contemporaries, fellow writers Cyril Dabydeen and Arnold Itwaru. After she left school she went to work as a journalist in Georgetown. She attended the University of Guyana between 1968-1970. She began writing in the mid 1960s and in 1974 she was a prizewinner in the N.H.A.C Literary Competition.

In 1970 she moved to London where she still lives. She did postgraduate literary studies at the University of London. In addition to her work as an author, she has also worked in London as an editor for several journals, as a political and cultural activist and as a college and university lecturer. She has done reading tours in North America, Europe, the Caribbean and Asia, and was a Visiting Fellow at New York University.

She has published three novels, *Timepiece* (Peepal Tree, 1986), *The Last English Plantation* (Peepal Tree, 1988) and *Chinese Women* (Peepal Tree, 2010).

She has been a regular reviewer of fiction, and her latest piece was a long essay on Zadie Smith's *White Teeth*, published in the academic journal *Small Axe*.

ALSO AVAILABLE

Timepiece

ISBN 9780948833038; pp. 206; 1986; 2011; £9.99

Sandra Yansen must leave behind the close ties of family and village when she goes away to take up a job as a reporter in Georgetown. But she feels that leaving Pheasant is a betrayal and is confused about where she stands in the quarrel between her mother Helen, who is pro-town and her father, Ben, who is deeply attached to the country and its values.

She finds the capital riven by racial conflict and the growing subversion of political freedom. Her newspaper has become the mouthpiece of the ruling party and she finds her ability to tell the truth as a reporter increasingly restricted. In the office she has to confront the chauvinism and vulnerability of her male colleagues whilst at the same time finding common cause with them in meeting the ambivalent challenges of Guyana's independence.

Yet, uncomfortable as she frequently is in the city, Sandra knows that she is growing in a way that Pheasant would not allow. But when Sandra is summoned home with the news that Helen is seriously ill, and re-encounters the enduring matriarchy of her mother's friends, Nurse, Miss K., Noor and Zena, she knows once again how much she is losing. It is their values that sustain Sandra in her search for an independence which does not betray Pheasant's communal strengths.

Fred D'Aguiar wrote of *Timepiece* 'recovering a valuable past for posterity and enriching our lives in the process' and Ann Jordan in *Spare Rib* reviewed it as 'not a novel to be taken at face value, for its joy lies in the fact that it works on so many different levels... the subtleties and tensions of life are not far from the surface as the author questions the notions of political as well as individual dependence and independence'. *Timepiece* won the 1987 Guyana prize.

The Last English Plantation
ISBN 9781900715331; pp. 182; 1988, 2001; £8.99

'So you want to be a coolie woman?' This accusation thrown at twelve year old June Lehall by her mother signifies only one of the crises June faces during the two dramatic weeks this fast-paced novel describes. June has to confront her mixed Indian-Chinese background in a situation of heightened racial tensions, the loss of her former friends when she wins a scholarship to the local high school, the upheaval of the industrial struggle on the sugar estate where she lives, and the arrival of British troops as Guyana explodes into political turmoil.

Merle Collins writes: 'Jan Shinebourne captures the language of movement, mime, silences, glances, with a feeling that comes from being deep within the heart of the Guyanese community. In *The Last English Plantation* her achievement lies in having the voices of the New Dam villagers dominate the politically turbulent period of 1950s Guyana – A wonderful and stimulating voyage into the lives behind the headlines, into the past that continues creating the changing present. The voices of the New Dam villagers never leave you.'

Wilson Harris writes: 'Jan Shinebourne's *The Last English Plantation* is set within a labyrinth of political chaos in British Guiana in the 1950s. But the novel is more subtly as well as obsessively oriented towards the psychological as well as the inner landscape of a colonial age. A gallery of lives depicted in *The Last English Plantation* is drawn from diverse strata of cultural legacies and inheritance. The desolations, the comedy of adversity, the contrasting moods of individual and collective character give a ritual, however incongruous, substance to the fate of a dying Empire.'

Chinese Women
ISBN 978184523154; pp. 94; 2010; £ 8.99

Pairing Caribbean wounds with the grievances of political Islam, this intriguing novel begins as a sad story of unrequited love on a Guyanese sugar estate that descends into the obsessive world of stalking and the temptations of Jihad. Told through the eyes of Albert Aziz, a Guyanese Indian Muslim, the story opens with his boyhood memory of falling from a tree and being badly injured, after which he develops a compelling attraction to a young Chinese girl, Alice Wong, who lives on the same sugar estate. Now, years later, Aziz is a highly paid engineer in the Canadian nuclear industry. Although he has a new and prosperous life, he still nurtures racial resentments about the way he was treated as a child and has become a supporter of radical Islam. He also begins to fixate again on Alice and tracks her down. He finds that she is divorced and living in England and asks her to marry him. Though Aziz is telling the story, it is clear that Alice's apprehension is slowly mounting as she fears the consequences of what might happen if she turns him down.